Bubba
Goes To
Alabama

A
Spiritual Journey

Cover design by ThomasMax
Edited by Lee Clevenger

ISBN Number 978-0-9788571-5-8
First Printing, May 2007
Second Printing, April 2010

Published by:

ThomasMax Publishing
P.O. Box 250054
Atlanta, GA 30325
404-794-6588
www.thomasmax.com

Bubba Goes To Alabama

A
Spiritual Journey

Kenneth David Mobley

ThomasMax

Your Publisher
For The 21st Century

ACKNOWLEDGEMENTS

My heartfelt thanks are extended to:

— my publisher and editor, Lee Clevenger, for making things painless and pleasurable, and for being so patient with the last-minute changes and rewrites

— Holly McClure, my literary agent, for her advice and direction

— my computer guru and proof reader, Leslie Boleman, who suggested that I invest in a dictionary

— my former New York Agent, David Jacobs, for years of support

— my longtime friend, Patti Snook, for her constant encouragement

— and the three women who have put up with me the longest, my sisters Sheila McNeill, who bought me a stack of legal pads and pencils one Christmas and told me to try writing a novel, Debbie Youngner, and my mother, Nora Lee Mobley.

for
Ricky Mobley,
poet, author, and brother,
who fought a courageous battle with cancer
and fell asleep in the arms of our Lord
on a quiet Sunday morning in April, 2006

Foreword

In the beginning God created the Heavens and the Earth. In six days He had created everything within, and when He saw what he had done, He was very pleased, so on the seventh day He rested, and when He awoke on the eighth day, He created Bubba.

Prologue

When He saw what He had done, He was very skeptical, but went about His business.

Bubba was rather slow in mind and speech. He was tall with black curly hair covering most of his body. His eyes were large and dark, the color of coal. His teeth had not formed correctly and were unpleasantly separated. His face gave the appearance it had been chiseled out of stone and wrapped with flesh. A large jaw, protruding cheekbones and slightly sunken eyes offset by a pair of lips that always formed a gentle smile. His arms were long and muscular like his legs, and very hairy. On each of his large hands, the small finger was missing. His stubby feet both lacked the two outer toes. The rest were webbed together like duck's feet that gave way to an awkward walk.

God had power over all the universe and could have corrected Bubba's defects, but after long and hard consideration, He was intrigued by Bubba, so He sent him out into the world just like he had been created. God had created a majestic and magnificent world and He thought Bubba would be a nice contrast to a perfect creation.

Bubba awoke from his deep transit sleep and squinted his eyes toward Heaven. He had a strange sensation he had descended from above, and was confused just how he awoke on the floor of the wet forest. He yawned, stretched his arms wide, and rested them on his chest. The strange beat of his heart made him raise himself up. He cocked his head, turning his ear toward the beat and positioned his hand once again over his heart. His thoughts were interrupted when a sparrow suddenly fluttered its wings in the tree above and flew away. His eyes followed the sparrow until it disappeared into the forest.

Bubba rubbed his arms, gave a heavy sigh, touched his feet and examined his fingers. He raised his index finger, turning it back and forth, studying it. He then put his finger inside his mouth, bit down hard, quickly removed it and let a painful sound slip from his lips. He rubbed his finger and looked at the teeth marks around his knuckle, and thought to himself, *I'll never do that again.* He rose to his feet, stretched his arms again and yawned.

His eyes focused on a small stream and waterfall. The sound of rushing water over the rocks stirred his curiosity. Bubba studied the strange substance for a moment before taking his first steps to the waterfall and kneeling down beside the stream. He instinctively dipped his hand into the substance, wet his lips and smiled for the first time before cupping his hands together for a drink. The sun stood directly overhead, casting a light across the stream, enough for Bubba to see his face in the water. He was startled at first and splashed away at the water but quickly realized the reflection was his own face. He looked closer, running his hand over his face, curious and amused, raising an eyebrow and giving a curious groan.

Bubba tasted the water, but before he could get a drink, he saw another face in the water. The growl of a black grizzly brought him quickly to his feet. Bubba turned and faced the bear, so close he could smell its foul breath. Bubba stood frozen while his arms and legs trembled. A chill fell down his spine. making the hairs on his neck stand straight.

The bear stood on its hind legs, growled and raised its razor-sharp claws. Bubba hesitated for a moment out of fear, turned and ran across the stream and climbed on top of a large rock resting on top of the waterfall.

In three graceful leaps, the bear was at the rock stretching his huge hind legs, pawing at Bubba's feet. The bear growled again, opening its mouth wide. Bubba looked into the grizzly's deep hungry eyes. Its mouth stood wide open and Bubba could see the saliva dripping from the sharp, pointed fangs.

The bear stood erect, planting its front paws on the rock. Bubba quickly picked up a stone at his feet, and with all his strength, drew back and hit the bear between its eyes. The bear fell backward, tumbling into the water, still alive but momentarily stunned by the blow. Before the bear could recover, Bubba jumped down and continued to hit the bear until it was dead. Bubba picked up the bear's lifeless paw and watched it drop into the shallow water without resistance, nudging the bear in its side with his index finger. When he was sure the bear was dead, he looked at the rock in his hand and raised it over his head in triumph before dragging the bear to land, where he ate his first meal.

Bubba rubbed his stomach and gave a loud belch. His eyes scanned the forest. It was thick with tall trees; the forest floor was full of heavy brush and vegetation. The tops of the tall trees formed an overhead canopy, blocking most of the sunlight. Only a slight hint of light filtered through the dark shadows of the forest.

Bubba picked up the rock, walked through the thick foliage and was startled when a covey of quail sprang up at his feet. He quickly raised the rock in a defensive gesture and groaned. His eyes searched the forest for perhaps another black bear. He gripped the rock in his hand and cautiously stepped through the heavy underbrush.

The woods were full of game and wildlife. A small herd of speckled deer leaped gracefully through the brush, flicking their white tails as they quickly disappeared. Bubba watched a brown hawk dive from the sky and into the shadows of the forest. The hawk caught a snake in its claws, disappearing back into the clouds.

Bubba then turned his ear toward the hollow knock of a woodpecker's beak against a tree, and farther up he observed a nest of vultures waiting patiently on the naked branches of a dying tree.

An uneasy feeling stirred inside, enough to make Bubba's stomach quiver. He could feel his heart beating now without touching his chest. He had drunk plenty of water from the spring but now his throat was dry and thirsty again. He wiped a trickle of sweat from his brow and moved slowly, his eyes cautiously shifting and focusing momentarily on a bumblebee circling around his head. He swatted at the bee and, with one quick move, caught it in his palm and squeezed it to death. Bubba yelled and shook his hand. The bee fell to the ground but left its stinger implanted in Bubba's hand. Bubba pricked the stinger from his palm, examining it and wondering how something so small could hurt so much. He rubbed his hand and gave a painful groan.

A few steps later he watched a legion of giant ants move in and out of a large mound of sand, and later stopped to observe a long yellow snake slide across the forest floor and disappear into the brush.

The experience, watching the inhabitants of the forest, was all too overwhelming for Bubba. For now, he thought to himself, they were all enemies, just like the bear that had attacked him, and the small bee that stung him. None could be trusted.

Bubba continued walking most of the afternoon. Soon the forest floor began to rise beneath his feet and he found himself climbing upward. His hands and feet were cut from the climb, but he continued up the hill, following a single beam of sunlight that cut through the treetops like a path leading to the mountain crest above. He followed the light to the top. When he reached the summit, a fading autumn sun was just dipping behind a dark valley of green below. He pulled himself up with both hands and then stood erect on a flat rock, arching his back, stretching his long arms. He took a deep breath of cool air, wiped the sweat from his eyes and focused his sight on the endless domain of woodlands that circled the summit; he could see nothing but miles and miles of dark forest.

A blanket of soft fog drifted overhead, slowly passing, and revealing a round, bright face that appeared to Bubba to be only an arm's reach away. Bubba stretched one arm high and spread his fingers, trying to grab the moon. He had no idea why he had walked all day with no destination and climbed toward the light, but this strange object that hung just out of reach, he thought, was somehow his reward for the hard climb. He had been in the light all day, and now the dark was something he didn't like. The dark had no life, like the sun and the sky. And the dark seemed to engulf him, closing the door to the world he had only known for a day.

A chilly wind swept across the mountaintop. Bubba experienced cold for the first time, groaned in discomfort, folded his arms together and squatted on the rock. He raised his eyes toward the light. The moonglow gave him a false sense of warmth and comfort. He studied the light for a few moments then leaped, springing from his feet like a frog, toward the moon in a futile attempt to grab it. In a split second Bubba found himself tumbling down the mountainside. He had leaped off the cliff, tumbled, fallen, and slid until his feet came to a rest against a tree, breaking his fall.

Momentarily stunned, Bubba uttered a painful groan, reached down and rubbed his knees which were cut and bleeding. He examined the red substance on the palm of his hand, dabbing a finger into the blood and tasting it, quickly spitting it out.

After regaining his composure, he carefully climbed down the mountain and began walking back to the spring. He walked most of the night until he found his birthplace. He then sat down next to the bear and had his second meal. After he finished, he ripped the hide off the bear and wrapped the fur side around him. He was tired from the climb and lay down on the wet ground, pulling the hide over his shoulders and resting his head against a clump of grass. His hand came to rest again on his heart. He felt it beat under his skin and wondered what he was doing in the forest all alone and how he got there. His eyes were heavy and tired. He listened to the howl of a wolf's cry in the distance wilderness. The forest came alive with strange sounds that echoed through the dark. He closed and opened his eyes, afraid to sleep for fear of the unknown, and weary of what lay ahead. Later, he fell asleep from exhaustion with the rock clutched tightly in his hand.

In a few months, Bubba learned the ways of survival. After the first heavy rainfall, he built a hut out of tree limbs and learned how to cut animal hide with sharp rocks for clothing. He discovered how to trap fish at the waterfall and catch thirsty animals when they came for water. He found that a club made from a tree was more deadly than a rock and soon realized the forest was not entirely a hostile environment, quickly learning who was friend or foe as he adapted to his surroundings.

One day lightning shot across the sky, catching a tree on fire. Bubba was no longer cold at night. He kept a flame burning until he learned how to rub sticks together to create fire.

Bubba made regular visits to the summit where he basked in the warm sun and search for other human life, often staying until dark and watching the moon and stars. He learned the four seasons and how to count the days, and how to cut meat and dry it during the summer months in preparation for the heavy snows that would come in the dreaded winter.

He had been living in the forest for almost three years when his discontent became overwhelming. He was lonely and his days filled with boredom and despair. He often looked at his own face in the water, splashing away at the reflection out of frustration and realized the time was coming to find his way out of the forest and search for another creature just like himself.

One spring day, he found a newborn hawk that had fallen from its nest. The bird was hardly bigger than the palm of his hand. He picked the bird up by its neck and dangled it before him. His first instinct was to eat the tender creature, but he had second thoughts. He often marveled at how the great birds soared high above earth and he was too excited to think about eating it. He thought, perhaps, he could learn how to fly by studying the bird so he decided to keep it.

He made a small cage for the hawk and nourished it daily with worms and insects. At night, he brought the cage inside his hut and let the bird out of its cage. He often fell asleep with it cradled in his arms. By fall the hawk was large enough to flap its wings. It had become so dependent on Bubba it no longer needed to be caged. Bubba often tossed the hawk into the air to help it fly, but the hawk was too young and fell back to the ground. Bubba watched young hawks soar overhead and was intrigued by how gracefully they glided with such ease over the currents of the skies. They were swift and fearless predators, snatching other smaller birds with lightening speed. Bubba wondered if his bird would be like the large hawks that flew overhead but was beginning to have doubts about his bird's ability to fly.

The hawk slept beside Bubba at night and stayed under his feet during the day. Bubba's speech was limited to grunts and incoherent syllables, but he began to communicate with the hawk. He named it Gork, a sound he often made while drinking water, and now Gork began to answer to his name. Bubba found Gork to be a good source of comfort and he worried Gork would fly away one day, and he did.

One morning Bubba awoke to find the hawk gone. He searched the forest all day but Gork was nowhere to be found. Bubba feared he might have strayed out of the hut during the night and fallen prey to a wolf, uncertain he could fly.

After two days and no sign of Gork, Bubba gave up hope. He lay down on his bed, thinking about how much he missed Gork. When he felt something wet on his cheeks, he touched the tear with his finger. He wiped his eyes and felt tears dripping down his cheeks. It felt good to release his emotions so Bubba continued crying for the first time.

Early the next morning while preparing to hunt, Bubba saw a hawk soaring high above. He had little hope it was Gork until each circle the hawk made brought it closer. When the hawk was just over the tree line, it swooped down and headed toward Bubba. Bubba held his arm up and Gork, with his wings wide open to break his speed, landed on Bubba's hand. Bubba was so overjoyed that later he and Gork shared a worm together for a snack.

Gork often left early in the morning and by dark he was back at the hut. Each afternoon Bubba looked forward to the hawk's coming home. One day Gork was gone for only a couple of hours when he returned with a small animal in his claws. When Bubba saw this he hurried over to the hut where Gork had placed the animal. Bubba could hardly believe it. Gork had caught a small newborn lion cub and had brought it home alive.

After placing the cub in front of the hut, Gork took flight back to the sky. Bubba wondered if Gork had

brought the cub for him, or if Gork was planning to eat
later. When he saw Gork feeding the cub a wild berry, h
realized Gork had brought the cub for him. He furthe
discovered Gork was a very special bird, unlike any bir
he had observed. He was larger than most hawks an
darker with white specks on his back and wingtips, and
solid white breast. His eyes were gray with a thin slice ͼ
silver running vertically through his black pupils, and h
beak and feet were yellow, the color of summer cori
Bubba often entertained the thought Gork was create
just like himself, out of nowhere.

Bubba fed the cub coconut milk, berries, and drie
beef. He knew by watching the wildlife in the forest tha
the first few weeks were very important for survival. H
built a cage for the cub and wrapped it in fur to keep
warm. One morning the cub broke out of his cage an
entered Bubba's hut while he was asleep. Bubba awok
to find the cub sitting on his hairy chest and playing wit
his beard. Bubba laughed. When he realized laughing fe
good, he laughed again.

Bubba developed a vocabulary of his own an
referred to the winds and the Heavens as Tonka, so Bubb
named the cub after the Heavens. He took Tonka on dail
swims in the spring and on morning hunts. Tonka, Gorl
and Bubba ate together, hunted together, and slept clos
to one another at night. Bubba talked to Tonka and Gor
and they listened to his every word as if they knew an
understood what he was saying . . . and perhaps they di
because they obeyed his every command.

One day while hunting, Bubba and Tonka cam
across a clan of lions. Bubba and Tonka lay in the thic
brush and watched the lions devour a young deer. Bubb
wondered if it was one of these lions that had given birtl
to Tonka. He looked at Tonka, stroking him gently on hi

growing mane. Tonka lay quietly, watching the lions. Bubba feared losing Tonka but nudged him to join the other lions if he wished, pointing his finger in the direction of the lions. Tonka raised his eyes at Bubba and then looked at the lions. He stood for a moment but quickly settled back into the tall grass. Tonka looked at Bubba and yawned, followed by a faint growl. A sign he did not like the lions. Bubba gave a nod of approval and smiled to himself. Gork was perched nearby in a tree, watching. Bubba and Tonka slipped quietly away from the lions and walked back to the hut with the confidence Tonka would never desert him.

Within a year Tonka grew to the stature of an adult lion. His thick mane was so long it fell over his eyes. Gork and Tonka played together, with Gork usually hovering just high enough above Tonka to stay out of his playful reach. If Gork wasn't flying, his favorite sitting spot was on Tonka's back or Bubba's shoulder.

Tonka and Gork became Bubba's family. He took them daily onto the summit where Bubba would sit for hours in hopes of spotting other creatures like himself. Bubba and Tonka would sit on the crest and enjoy watching Gork soar through the clouds. Often they stayed until dark and watched the stars. When they were ready to leave, a loud growl from Tonka would summon Gork to fly down and land on Bubba's shoulder and the three would begin their journey home.

* * * * *

The forest was calm, too still for Bubba. The usual sounds that filled the dark were more silent than most nights. Bubba awoke and walked outside his hut. He had been restless all night, and the stillness gave him reason to rise from his bed. A full moon stood directly overhead. His eyes found the evasive object, and he gave a dissatisfied grunt. The moon always reminded him of his fall down the mountain, and especially so when it was full. Tonight it was unusually bright. The treetops wore a crown of light, and the moonbeams pounced off the spring.

Bubba shifted his eyes toward the Heavens. A gentle wind stirred the thin branches of the treetops. The trees awoke and began to sing from the breeze, giving life to the dark. The crickets and frogs soon joined the ensemble, bringing music and harmony to the woods. The thin branches of the trees against the gray sky reminded Bubba of small fingers reaching upwards, pleading with the Heavens. Bubba watched the treetops for a moment and fell into a deep depression.

Bubba walked to the spring, knelt down, and looked at his reflection. It was the same spot where he had killed the bear on his first day on earth. But now thought he would have been better off if the bear had killed him. He was tired of living alone and could only think of dying. He brought his hand to his throat and squeezed it until he felt faint. His suicide attempt was interrupted by a gentle growl from Tonka. Bubba turned and saw Tonka standing behind. Tonka wagged his tail and sat beside Bubba. In a moment, Gork was nearby, fluttering his wings like a peacock and strutting around. Bubba raised a pair of sad eyes at Tonka and Gork.

Tonka purred and licked Bubba's hand. It was as if they had come to rescue him, and perhaps they had. They always seemed to know when Bubba was happy or sad, and tonight they had obviously sensed something was very wrong.

Bubba realized what a foolish thing he had just done,

and how much his animals loved him. He decided he had to leave the dark forest.

* * * * *

At the beginning of summer, Bubba left his home of six years with Gork and Tonka to begin his journey. Bubba had never traveled more than a few days' walk from the hut but was prepared for the challenge. The summer offered plenty of fresh fruit, easy game, and little shelter was needed at night. Bubba figured he would be out of the forest by fall but by the end of summer they were still surrounded by trees. They traveled mostly at night, following the North Star, but often bad weather hid the guiding star behind the clouds.

By the end of fall they were still in the forest and Bubba feared the cold winter months ahead. He walked day and night and often lost his way because of bad weather. When the first snow fell they were still in the forest. Meat was hard to find during winter so they survived on very little rations. Eventually the snow became too deep for travel, and Bubba was forced to build a hut and stay put for the winter. It was a very trying time for Bubba, Tonka, and Gork, staying in such close quarters together for over three months where they could only sleep and eat.

The beginning of spring offered new hope, but by the end of the next fall, they had made little progress. Bubba and his friends endured another harsh winter, and another one after that. They had been traveling in the forest for almost three years, and Bubba was quickly giving up hope of finding his way out. Navigating the deep woods without reference points became very frustrating. There were times after a week of walking he found himself right back where he had begun, realizing he had walked in a circle. He wondered if this vast land was nothing but forest.

One day Bubba stopped walking and sat down with Tonka by his side. He stroked Tonka and gave a heavy sigh. Tonka yawned and rolled over in the grass. He, too, was tired and weary from traveling. Bubba decided he couldn't go any farther. Perhaps he was the only creature in the world like himself, he thought. And the dark forest was all that existed. He decided to give up his search and make a new home where he sat. It was then he heard a strange sound overhead. He looked up and saw hundreds of birds flying above the treetops. They were solid-white birds with golden beaks, birds he had never seen.

Gork emerged from the flock of birds and landed next to Bubba with one of the birds clenched in his claws. Bubba realized his journey had come to an end. This was not a bird that lived in the dark forest. Bubba stood and walked a short distance to a cliff at the edge of the forest. He felt the warm sun against his face. The air was fresh and cool and he took a deep breath, followed by a heavy sigh. He marveled at the body of water the size of a thousand springs and roared like a den of hungry lions. The earth was covered with white sand and stretched as far as he could see.

Bubba climbed down from the jagged cliff and walked toward the water. Tonka growled and dashed toward the ocean, stopping just short of the water, turning his head at Bubba, wagging his tail and panting. Bubba motioned Tonka to wait, but he was already galloping into the surf.

Bubba laughed aloud and removed the worn leather wraps around his feet and waded in the surf. He watched Tonka run along the beach. Gork was soaring low over the ocean, teasing the other birds, snipping at their tail feathers.

The sun dipped below the blue of the ocean, casting a rainbow across the horizon, creating a perfect sunset. The sound of the roaring ocean was music Bubba had never heard. The taste of salt in the air, the gentle breeze . . . it was all too soothing.

Bubba lay back on the soft beach, resting his head on the sand. Overhead a thousand stars filled the Heavens. Bubba lay on his back watching the sky and nodding his head in approval. Tomorrow, he thought, he would search for other creatures like himself. But for now he would sleep well for the first time in many years.

* * * * *

The following morning Bubba looked east and west at the long stretch of beach sand. Gork was flying to the west, so that was the direction Bubba chose to begin his journey. They camped along the way, and Bubba discovered a new diet of clams and sea turtles, but there were no sign of other human beings. He looked for footprints in the sand that might resemble his own but after a full month of walking, no other footprints were found. Bubba and Tonka walked the beach for almost a season and until they came to a junction where the forest met the sea, only separated by a narrow cliff. Bubba climbed the cliff to find the beach had disappeared, and there was nothing but miles of jagged cliffs, against a wall of tall dark woods. He was trapped between the forest and the ocean.

Bubba pitched a hut at the edge of the forest and stayed for almost a week while deciding what to do. One day he picked up a stick and pushed it beneath the water

and watched it quickly come to the top. Bubba saw this
and built a raft out of palm logs, making rope from tree
strips and tying the logs together. In a matter of a few
days the crude raft was completed. After he gathered
food and water for the journey, he and his animals
hitched a ride on the first big wave and drifted out to sea.

Bubba stood on the raft and took his last look at the
dark forest. He hoped he would never have to return.
Just to look at the sun and feel the warm rays beam down
on his face was something he had never experienced. The
sea gave him a sense of hope and freedom he had never
known and whatever lay ahead would have to be better
than his lonely days in the forest.

The giant whale rose high out of the sea. The sudden burst to the surface of the calm seas startled Bubba and brought Tonka to his feet. But the whale quickly submerged, leaving only a ripple as the sea swallowed him. When they spotted the whale again, it was far out, but within moments it surfaced close to the raft, almost tipping it over. It then slowly sank into the sea, then re-surfaced and swam alongside of the raft, spouting seawater high into the air and flapping its dorsal tail in a playful gesture. Bubba and Tonka stood in awe and watched the big fish swim alongside the raft.

Numerous times it dove back into the sea and surfaced alongside the raft. Bubba reached down and stroked Tonka's thick mane, a sign this giant creature was friendly. Tonka sat down, resting on his legs, and watched the whale. The whale turned its huge dark eyes on Bubba, who thought to himself the fish was trying to speak to him. The giant saucer-like eyes of the whale looked lonely and searching, but friendly. Bubba felt a calm, soothing energy from the whale and knew the giant fish was his friend. He had no fear of the whale. He reached out and touched the whale, stroking its side very gently. The whale slowly closed and opened its eyes like it was saying goodbye and slowly submerged. Bubba and Tonka waited and watched for the whale to rise again. It rose just in front of the raft a final time. His giant gray tail lifted out of the water and came back down, showering Bubba and Tonka before disappearing.

Bubba thought about the whale for many days. He had found a friend in the sea just like he had found Tonka and Gork in the dark forest. He wished the whale would return to ease the long and boring days but it never did.

The sea, however, was not as friendly as the whale. The mornings were normally calm but in the afternoons the sky often turned dark and twisted like a snake pouring down its venom. They endured fierce thunderstorms that tossed and lifted the raft like a leaf torn from its branches and twirling in the wind.

There were days when time stood still and they drifted with nothing but the slow sound of rippling water to keep them awake. The sun was both their enemy and friend. They welcomed the sun after a cold windy night but hated the sun when they begin to thirst for water. The wind was the same. It was also their friend or their enemy. It kept the raft moving but in a second it could turn deadly, twisting into a dark funnel. The force of the wind and the salty air blistered his eyes and cut through his skin like a razor knife.

Gork flew low above the sea each day searching for a lazy fish to catch. But the farther out to sea they drifted, the scarcer the food became. Soon there were no more birds in sight, no fish to catch, no sea turtles to eat.

After two weeks at sea, they were out of food and water. Tonka had a big appetite, unlike Bubba and Gork; he needed more to survive. The sun left them exhausted at the end of each day, and the nights were cold and windy. In another week Bubba's hands and lips split open and bled. When there was no rainwater to catch, Tonka could only lie down and pant from thirst. Gork caught an occasional fish, but his catches were hardly enough to keep them alive.

Bubba wondered if he had made the right decision. He had put his beloved animals at risk for his own selfish needs and now he deeply regretted it. Tonka's bones were showing through his ribcage and even Gork could not fight the heavy winds that stirred the skies. Bubba gave what little rainwater that was caught to Tonka with little thought to his own thirst. In another week, skin was hanging off Bubba's bones, and he and Tonka were close to death. The constant movement of the raft, the deprivation and the exposure caused Bubba to hallucinate and he drifted in and out of reality. His vivid dreams took him to places in his mind he never knew existed, and it took all his mental strength to concentrate on a single thought.

One morning he was showered by a fresh rain and was able to catch enough water to survive another day. After he and Tonka drank the water, Bubba raised his eyes toward the Heavens and cried out. Every beast in the forest, every bird, even the lizard and the insects, he thought, had offspring like themselves; and each one had a mate and they always multiplied. He had watched the animals of the dark forest mate several times and give birth. Yes, he thought to himself, someone, somewhere, must have given birth to him. He felt certain for the first time that someone or something greater existed.

He remembered when he first awoke in the forest and raised his eyes toward the Heavens. He couldn't remember why he had done so, he just had. *I was created from above*, he thought, and this revelation greatly renewed his strength. With all the strength he could gather, Bubba raised himself up on his knees, looked toward the Heavens and cried out again for help. He spread one arm toward the Heavens and pointed a single finger at Tonka as if to show God Tonka was dying.

Overhead the sky turned dark and the winds gathered speed. The sky roared with thunder and lighting struck the water so close, the hairs on his arms stood straight. Bubba looked to the skies and saw Gork flying just below the clouds with a rodent in his claws. Bubba quickly regained hope. He knew Gork had been gone for a day and a night and land had to be nearby.

But now the seas rose like a volcano beneath him and the sun disappeared behind the clouds. Bubba heard a loud roar and raised his eyes to a wall of water tall as a mountain, coming directly at him. He reached over and held onto Tonka, who lay motionless. The giant wave raised the raft higher than any tree in the dark forest, and with the strength of a savage beast forced the raft back down on the water so hard it split into pieces.

Bubba found himself below the water and when he surfaced he yelled out for Tonka. The wave raised him up high but within a split second he felt himself falling, plummeting into a deep valley between the waves. When the wave lifted him again, he could see Tonka not far away and swam toward him. Before he could reach Tonka, his strength gave out and his arms and legs became lifeless. Suddenly under water with little strength left, he held his breath until his lungs seemed to explode. The strong surface wind pushed the water down, making it impossible for him to surface. When Bubba could hold his breath no longer, he felt himself moving upward and opened his eyes and realized Tonka was pulling him. When they surfaced, Bubba took a deep breath and grabbed onto Tonka's mane.

Within minutes the sea calmed and a ray of sunlight filtered through the clouds. The storm left quickly as it had come. The winds had carried them toward the shore and Bubba could see land. He held onto Tonka's mane until he felt the earth beneath his feet. He and Tonka struggled onto the shore and collapsed.

When Bubba awoke that afternoon, a strange creature with a long neck, funny looking legs, and a hump on his back was standing over him. Bubba came to his knees and bowed to the camel. When the camel snared and drooled on Bubba, Bubba quickly came to his feet and realized this odd creature was not the unseen one which had saved them from the sea. Tonka quickly arose. One loud roar chased the camel away.

Bubba was pleased to find Gork nearby feasting on a freshly caught desert rat. Bubba and Tonka were tired and hungry. After a short walk they found a large spring surrounded by palms and coconut trees. Later that day, Tonka was able to catch a stray goat drinking from the spring. Bubba built a fire, and the two ate their first good meal in weeks.

Bubba and Tonka rested by the spring for several days. There was no shortage of good food. Late at night and early morning, rodents from the desert would come to drink from the spring where Tonka would be hiding and waiting.

While Bubba regained his strength, he thought about his journey across the sea and how he and his friends had almost died, and only when he cried out for help were they saved. Although he could not see this creature that saved him, he was certain he existed. The thought renewed Bubba's hopes, and he was more determined than ever to find the one responsible for saving him.

After Bubba and Tonka rested, Bubba prepared for their journey across the desert. He walked a short distance from the spring and looked across the endless miles of rolling sand. The sand dunes reminded him of the ocean waves without water. The winds blowing atop the sand gave the illusion the sand was moving like the waves. To Bubba, the desert looked like a sea on fire.

He knew it would not be an easy trip. The dark forest, the unforgiving sea . . . his entire existence had been a challenge, and he mentally prepared for the days, months, or years ahead. The sea was a voyage of self-discovery and inner strength. Bubba realized his mind had to be as strong as his body; both were important for survival.

While resting at the spring, he watched the camel drink from the opposite side in the early morning hours. If he could catch this strange creature, he thought, the supplies could be carried on the animal's back.

Bubba made a rope out of tree bark as he had done to build the raft. He formed a large loop at one end and a small loop, which he tied around his wrist. When the camel arrived at daybreak Bubba and Tonka were hiding behind a large rock, patiently waiting. Bubba caught the camel by surprise and quickly threw the loop around its neck.

The camel was stubborn and also fast on its feet. It galloped away dragging Bubba helplessly across the desert sand. Bubba held onto the rope while he bounced across the desert floor. Tonka ran beside the camel trying to make it stop but the camel continued across the desert until it finally tired and came to a stop and sat down on all four legs.

The remainder of the afternoon was spent getting the camel to its feet. When it finally stood, Bubba led the camel back to the spring, loaded the supplies on the camel's back and mentally prepared himself for the challenge that lay ahead.

The journey across the desert was harsh, but nothing could compare with the raging sea and the dark forest. The days were hot, and Bubba was often blinded by the reflection of the sun off of the desert sand. The blistering heat and the scorched sand felt like a hot bed of coals, but Bubba was happy to have the earth beneath him. It gave him a sense of security he did not have when at the mercy of the sea. Crossing the high ridges of sand reminded him of walking in the deep snow of the dark forest. The earth sank beneath his feet, and many times he found himself knee-deep in sand. The sound of the howling wind was like a wolf's cry and often signaled a sandstorm was imminent. Bubba would gather the animals in a circle and lie down on the hot floor of the desert until it passed. When it was over they would have to dig themselves out of the sand. To Bubba, it was like being covered with a thick hot blanket and being buried alive under the scorching sand.

The desert air was dry, much different from the air at sea. Bubba had the sensation he was being cooked from the inside out. His lungs constantly hurt, and the simple act of swallowing with a dry throat was difficult and painful. But the cool water from an occasional spring temporarily eased the suffering until they ran out of water again.

And, Bubba realized, without the camel's help, the journey would be impossible. He learned how to mount and ride the camel. The large hump on the camel's back was an obstacle he eventually mastered, and he wondered what purpose such a thing could have. The camel was stubborn but Bubba was very affectionate with the animal, and soon it was tamed. He named it Cocoa, and the camel began responding to his name.

Gork found plenty of rats and lizards for dinner. Each night before Bubba fell asleep he thanked this unseen creature for saving their lives. He watched the stars in Heaven at night and wondered if he had fallen from one of the stars. Perhaps it was only a matter of time before he was rescued.

Hope kept Bubba going. Without it, Bubba realized he would have perished in the dark forest or at sea. Hope was like food and water, it was essential to survival.

* * * * *

After a year of battling the scorching desert, Bubba saw tree lines in the distance. He remembered the tricks played on his mind by the sea and hoped it was not another illusion. Nevertheless, his spirits were lifted, and he dismounted Cocoa and hurried toward a barren mountain. Upon reaching the top, he folded his hand over his eyes to block the sun and to get a better view. He laughed aloud, stretching his arms above his head, clenching his fist in excitement. In the distance was a large winding river, opening up into a vast blue sea. Beyond lay countryside blanketed with colorful trees and green grass. Bubba's excitement was hard to contain. He dashed down the mountain, jumped onto Cocoa, and gave a forward motion to Tonka and Gork. Sensing something good was happening, Tonka let out a loud roar and ran alongside Cocoa.

By sunset Bubba approached the great river and found himself walking on grass, not sand. Ahead, nestled between the comfort of palms, was a fresh-water spring, and beyond he marveled at the majestic cliffs and rolling hills, all adorned with the colors of spring. The sea gave birth to the river, which cut its path through the cliffs and hills, splintering like fingers into different directions.

At last Bubba felt he had reached his destination. The riverbanks were lined with tall palms and beautiful trees unlike any Bubba had ever seen, and the fresh smell of grass and flowers at his feet was something he had never experienced. He stopped, took a deep breath and enjoyed the aroma of new life that filled the air. Bubba smiled and nodded his head in approval.

He decided he would travel no farther and make his home where he stood. He had not given up hope of finding another like himself or searching for one who had saved him from the sea but, he was too tired to continue his travels.

While Tonka was rolling in the grass and Gork was perched high in a tree, studying a flock of geese soaring overhead, Bubba knelt for a drink of water. He looked at his reflection and ran his hand across his face, which appeared different than it had in the dark forest. His hair was whiter, and his eyes seem to sink beneath a darker skin. As he studied his face he realized something inside of him had also changed. He felt a new peace and contentment. He didn't understand why, he just did. Perhaps it was the satisfaction of victory over nature, a sense of triumph, or the fact he and his friends had survived the long odyssey. He was happy he had found a home and was at peace with himself.

Bubba dipped his hands into the spring, bringing the water to his lips. He paused momentarily, looked over his shoulder, smiled to himself — remembering the episode in the dark forest — and laughed. There was not a black bear in sight.

Suddenly, a voice surrounded him, and he raised himself up, darting his eyes left and right.

"He that drinks from the water of life will never thirst again," said the voice.

Bubba was blinded by a beautiful light that pierced and radiated through every bone in his body. He fell to his knees and trembled in fear until he felt a warm glow swell inside. He instantly knew the light was a friend.

"Who are you?" Bubba thought to himself.

"Hear my words and you will henceforth understand. I am the living God, the One that created you and much better looking than the camel."

It was the first time Bubba had experienced humor. It made him relaxed, as though he was in the presence of a good friend, although he had never had one other than his animals.

"Most have misconceptions about me," said God. "I'm really not dull at all. Humor and laughter are good medicine for the heart and soul."

"I have traveled very far to find you," said Bubba.

"I have been right here all the while," replied God, "and I came when you called my name, though you did not know me."

"Thank you for saving my friends," replied Bubba.

"It was you, Bubba, through your unselfish acts of love that you and your friends were saved. When I created you I had my doubts. I've done better jobs. But against great odds you have survived and grown in the ways of God and of man. You were a quick study, and with you I am well pleased."

"But I did little but roam the forest most of my existence," replied Bubba.

"On the contrary, Bubba," said God. "You have done very much in your short time on earth. It only took a small bird to make you cry and little kitten to make you laugh. Many of my creatures at your stage of existence do neither. Emotional development is very important to your growth, and by the way, it was not you who tamed the animals, but the animals that tamed you. I have to give credit where credit is due. Your kindness and devotion to your small friends showed you are capable of great love and compassion."

"What about the bear?" asked Bubba.

"I'm going to overlook that one," said God. "But now on with the story, I have a heavy workload today. The fact you found your way out of the forest showed you had determination which is essential in life to accomplish great deeds. You have many good traits, but what impressed me the most were two things that are very rare. You asked me to save your animals and spoke nothing of yourself. And you gave them food and water when you needed it just as much. It was a very unselfish act and when you tried to save Tonka, and, well, that took the cake, like some of my creatures say. Courage is a very rare trait in most of my mortal creatures."

"I rarely make personal appearances," continued God, "but I couldn't miss this one. In you, Bubba, I see great promise and good things to come."

"Is there another like me, God?"

"Yes, Bubba," answered God. "I created you in my likeness in that my spirit prevails within you and all my creatures. And I did not create man to live alone but first hear my words and write them on the tablets of your heart. There are many good traits that are essential in developing good character and personality. My seven favorites   are   humor,   kindness,   compassion, determination, courage, unselfishness, and love. You have mastered these traits and done very well. One day you will teach these qualities to others but first there are other lessons you must learn."

"I see you have a request," said God.

"How did you know when I said nothing?" replied Bubba

"That is why many call me the all-knowing God, Bubba. I never miss a beat, like some of my mortals say. Even the hairs on your head are numbered and I knew you even before I created you."

"Where are other creatures like myself?" asked Bubba. "I have searched everywhere."

"This is a vast domain, Bubba. I find it impossible to think small. And yes, there are many similar to you but none exactly like you. None of my mortals think alike, act alike or look alike. But I'm working on the look-alike thing; and the fact all my mortals are different makes my creation very unique."

"Where would I find such a creature?"

"She is in transit as we speak. The angels in Heaven stand ready to obey my every thought."

"I have waited a long time to feel the touch of another creature similar to me," replied Bubba.

"Your request is well deserved. Never will you be lonely again. A little miserable at times, perhaps, but you'll never be lonely or have a dull moment again. She is a woman and her name is Lucy. She is a good match for you, I hope. But that is up to you and her. I try not to interfere with relationships. I have more important things to do with my time. But we shall talk again. You shall then tell me all about Lucy. Now I must leave, Bubba. My love be with you."

"Must you go?" asked Bubba

"Humbleness is another trait, I adore, Bubba. You are certainly full of surprises. I must go bask in my own glory, that I have created something like you."

"May I ask just two questions?

"Yes, Bubba. But make them quick. I am very busy."

"Why do you call me Bubba?"

"You awoke next to a bubbling spring, and I thought it appropriate."

"Hmmm," Bubba moaned, scratching his chin with his fingers.

"And your other question?" asked God.

"I want to know why you put the hump on the camel's back?"

"Now I ask you, Bubba . . . why not?"

Bubba raised an eyebrow, contemplating the wisdom of such an answer.

"It is good you ponder such thoughts. It shows your mind will quickly develop. That was a very good question. Now peace be unto you."

The great and beautiful light faded. God returned to Heaven and after He had rested He awoke on the ninth day and He created Lucy.

When He saw what he had done He was very curious and went about his business.

Lucy was still asleep from her transit voyage. She was lying peacefully under a palm when the light of God faded. Bubba's excitement was hard to contain. He had traveled very far to find this woman but now he was hesitant. He had conquered fear over the savage beast of the forest but now he felt his hands trembling in anticipation as he slowly made his way to her. He wasn't sure how she would react or what he should do first. If this woman came from God, he thought, it would be a creature very similar as God had promised. God had brought him all this way and certainly this thing God called woman would be perfect, just like him, so he thought.

Bubba's eyes traveled up and down Lucy's body and focused on her soft white garment. He studied her long brown hair, lifting it gently with his fingers. After smelling her hair he uttered a disapproving grunt at the unpleasant odor. To him it smelled like fresh fruit and berries. Her skin was whiter and smoother than his. She was much smaller than Bubba, something he hadn't expected. And her body had more curves and shapes. Bubba looked at her feet and counted her toes. There were way too many, he thought. He then counted her fingers and then counted his own. He shook his head and gave a sigh of dissatisfaction. He wondered why God would send him such an imperfect creature.

Bubba quietly moved around Lucy to look at her face. He squatted, moving his head left and right, observing her unblemished skin. She had no facial hair and her lips were full and slightly parted at the top. Bubba gently parted her lips for a look at her teeth. When he saw they were narrow and straight, he let out a loud angry grunt, enough to awaken Lucy.

Lucy opened her eyes and saw Bubba kneeling beside her. Before Bubba could react, Lucy sprang to her feet, drew back and punched Bubba between the eyes. Bubba fell backwards and before he could get to his feet Lucy was gone. A knot quickly swelled between his eyes the size of a small bird egg. He gave a painful grunt and motioned toward the Heavens.

When the great light of God appeared, Bubba gave an anguished smile, and dropped to his knees.

"Yes, Bubba," said God. "This is almost a first for me, coming to the aid of a creature in a domestic situation. What is the problem?"

"With all respect, Lord, you already know the problem," responded Bubba. "She is nothing like me. She has way too many toes and fingers, her hair smells like fruit, and she hit me between the eyes. I have a lump on my head."

"Yes, Bubba, I can see," answered God. "First of all Bubba, have you considered the fact it is you that may have too few fingers and toes?"

Bubba looked down at his toes and counted his fingers.

"And perhaps it is you," continued God, "that needs

to bathe in the stream so your hair may also smell like fresh fruit."

Bubba scratched his head and squinted his eyes, contemplating God's response.

"You have learned a valuable lesson," continued God. "Never judge another by your own standards. It was a match made in Heaven, with no pun intended, so never doubt the wisdom of my choice."

"But she hit me between the eyes, Lord"

"And that is another lesson," said God. "You asked to feel the touch of another creature. So be careful what you shall ask for. You just may receive your wishes. Now I must go. These are problems only you can resolve. My matters concern those of my kingdom. There will probably be more lumps on your head until you understand the ways of a woman, and I am not here for such trivial matters. Now peace be unto you."

The great light of God vanished, leaving Bubba to think about the wisdom of God's words. Bubba spent the rest of the day in deep thought. He realized he must never call upon God again unless it concerned spiritual matters. Afterwards he turned his thoughts to Lucy. She wasn't the woman he expected. He would have to train her like he had done with Tonka and Gork. But first, he thought, she would need food, water and shelter.

He spent the afternoon making a small hut beside the spring and later built a fire to cook a meal of freshly caught fish. After finishing, he left in search of Lucy. Tonka quickly picked up her scent, and within moments he and Tonka were standing at the entrance to a cave. Bubba did his best to coax Lucy into coming outside. When she refused, Bubba dragged her outside by her arm and tied her on top of Cocoa. Lucy kicked and screamed, biting Bubba on the hand. Bubba gave Lucy a disgruntled eye and let out angry grunt, showing her he meant business, but the ploy had little effect on Lucy. She continued to resist.

Bubba returned to the hut and placed Lucy on the sand close to the fire. Her hands and feet were bound. She struggled with her restraints while Bubba moved about, preparing dinner, seemingly unconcerned she was so enraged. To Bubba, she was like a wild beast that needed to be trained, and he considered the restraints necessary.

Bubba removed a portion of fish, eating some himself to show Lucy how tasty it was. When he tried to feed Lucy she turned her head, refusing to open her mouth, snarling at Bubba so hard that her nose wrinkled and twitched. Bubba raised his shoulders, then let them fall with a deep exhale and gave an exasperating sigh. He handed Lucy's portion of the fish to Tonka, who quickly gulped it down. Bubba turned his eyes at Lucy and smirked. *I'll show you,* he thought.

Bubba left Lucy alone the remainder of the night. He made sure to keep the fire burning so that she would remain warm. Spring had not thoroughly divorced winter and a chilly breeze drifted over the river.

* * * * *

The day was breaking over the sea while Lucy slept. Bubba walked along the seashore with Tonka for the most part of the night, confused and troubled over Lucy. At the mouth of the river inlet, large rocks formed a jetty that stretched toward the sea. Bubba sat on top of the rocks watching the morning sun filter through the dark. A flock of seagulls were feeding over the water, and the familiar sounds of awakening fowl filled the air.

Bubba and Tonka lifted their eyes toward the sky at the first sign of Gork flying above. Watching Gork and the other birds fly freely above the earth Bubba realized he had to free Lucy. He bowed his head and prayed for the first time. He wasn't sure how to convey his thoughts in a way that would please God, so he talked to God like he talked to his animals: with devotion and sincerity. He asked God to help him make the right choices concerning Lucy. God might not appear in person, but Bubba knew God heard his prayer, and he felt better for praying. Little did he know God had already answered before he prayed.

Bubba returned to the hut and cut Lucy's straps from her hands and feet. She quickly stood, picked up a piece of firewood nearby, and hit Bubba over the head before running away. Bubba rubbed the top of his head and gave another painful grunt. He now had two matching lumps, one between his eyes and one on the top of his head.

Bubba lay awake that night thinking about the knots on his head. Lucy's reaction was something he hadn't expected. Doing the right thing, he thought, had only produced another lump on his head but he was glad he had made the right choice.

He thought about his long journey in search of another like himself and wondered why he was subject to more suffering, especially when she had been sent by his friend, God. He was very confused about this creature called woman. He had overcome great odds in the forest, at sea, and on the desert, but now he realized, his greatest challenge was asleep in her cave.

Bubba tossed and turned most of the night and fell asleep with no answers, concluding he had to be patient and wait.

The following day Bubba brought food and water to Lucy and left it outside her cave. When he returned the following day, it was gone. He continued this for several days and each day Lucy came of her cave to eat and drink.

A full moon brought an early spring tide to Bubba's doorsteps. He decided to relocate his hut farther from the sea. Behind him were flat woodlands and brush that gradually gave rise to the hills. Above the hills were high cliffs, and below were numerous caves and caverns. On the highest hill he built a larger hut and made Lucy a bed of leaves and bird feathers. He decorated the inside of the hut with colorful rocks and seashells.

* * * * *

A pale western sky was fading into the sunset when Bubba and Tonka reached the top of the cliff above the hut. He was curious about what lay beyond the cliff and found a trail leading to the top. To the west of the cliff lay miles of flat, barren land and beyond, a mountain range. Looking down, he watched the river twist like a snake between the cliffs. The sound of rushing waters echoed throughout the countryside.

Bubba sat down on a large rock balancing on the edge of the cliff. That rock would become his favorite spot for the remainder of his life. The rock was surrounded by tall grass and short, stubby trees with their tops shaved at an angle from the constant wind from the sea. The cliff brought back the memories of the early days on the summit in the dark forest where he could see for miles around and watch the stars unfold at night.

Now he watched Gork fly out over the vast sea, spreading his great and beautiful wings and soar against the sunset. The cliff became a place of solace, refuge and peace for Bubba . . . a place where he could pray and enjoy the beauty of God's creation.

* * * * *

One morning after Bubba and Tonka had been hunting, they returned to the hut and found Lucy sitting outside. It was hard for Bubba to stop grinning. He was careful not to approach her for fear she would run away. He decided to keep his distance until they developed a trust.

Lucy found her own club and held it up for Bubba to see as he walked by. She shook the club at Bubba and gave a triumphant grunt. Bubba pretended to ignore her. He walked to the spring for a drink of water and watched Lucy out of the corner of his eye only to see Lucy keeping a cautious eye on him.

Later that evening, Bubba cooked clams over a hot bed of coals while Lucy watched. He opened the first clam, and offered it to Lucy. She took the clam and quickly swallowed it, holding out her hand for another. Bubba was happy to accommodate her and fed Lucy clams until she let out a loud belch.

Bubba found wild berries fruits he had never tasted along the riverbanks. He discovered clay below the surface of the river and learned to mold and fashion the clay into pots and cookware. He squeezed grapes and berries into juice and made several pots full of tasty liquids, sauces and seasonings.

When Lucy had finished eating, Bubba handed her a cup of juice made from berries that had been fermenting in the sun for over a week. Lucy tasted the juice, gave an approving nod, and drank all the juice. She wiped her chin and held out her cup for more. Bubba refilled her cup. After drinking another two cups of juice Lucy began grunting and groaning. She laughed out loud for the first time, dancing around the fire, jumping up and down, flapping her arms like a bird and chirping. Gork observed Lucy for a few moments with a curious eye and flapped his wings and squawked. Bubba was both startled and amazed by the sudden transformation. Tonka rested his head on his paws, his eyes following Lucy while she danced around the campfire, uttering strange sounds. She reminded Bubba of a wiggling fish out of water . . . and at the same time a frog, jumping up and down, leaping around the fire. In a few moments, Lucy flopped down hard on her buttocks as though someone had pushed her, let out a loud belch, grunted, and then fell back into the ground. Her eyes slowly rolled under her eyelids, and she began snoring.

Bubba looked at Gork and Tonka as though he expected them to comment. His eyes traveled back to Lucy as she lay sprawled out on next to the fire. Bubba stood, walked to Lucy and squatted beside her. Tonka rose, moved beside Lucy and sniffed her body. Bubba lifted her arm and let it fall lifelessly to the ground. He then put his hand over her heart, felt a beat and smiled, relieved she was still breathing. He then smelled Lucy's cup and tasted the residue inside. Lucy's reaction was a total puzzle to Bubba. He had never drunk but a sip of the juice and wondered why Lucy would have such a reaction to it. Bubba wasn't happy with Lucy's strange behavior and vowed he would never give her juice again.

Bubba covered Lucy with a soft animal hide and stuffed it comfortably around her. He looked again at her face as she lay with her arms and legs spread wide and her eyes half parted. He hoped she would not awaken while he ran his finger down her cheek and across her face. His finger came to rest on her chin, and he tilted her face to the side, studying it for the first time without interruption. Her eyes were blue, like the sky but even bluer. Bubba put his finger on her nose and ran his finger down it. Her nose delicately sloped between a set of perfect eyes, high cheekbones and below rested a set of full and beautiful pink lips. He picked up her hand and closely examined her delicate fingers, one by one, and gave an approving grunt. He suddenly realized how beautiful Lucy was, and it was he who was imperfect. He raised his hand, closing his fingers until they made a hard fist. He hit himself on the side of his head. After studying Lucy for a few more moments, he hit himself again, this time harder.

The experience of falling in love was too overwhelming for Bubba and he hit himself again for being so stupid. And the fear the love would not be returned and his previous treatment of Lucy brought a sense of guilt, something he had ever experienced. It was the first time Bubba experienced a dislike for himself. He fell asleep that night more confused than ever, watching the reflection of Lucy lying by the dying embers of the fire.

Lucy showed up earlier each day and enjoyed watching Bubba make pottery, grind herbs, fish, or prepare food for dinner. She became friends with Tonka and Gork, learning their names, and they began responding to her commands. She took Tonka out each morning for a walk on the beach where she would gather seashells, conches and clams for dinner. When she caught a small fish, she enjoyed holding it over her head and watching Gork swoop down and snatch the fish from her fingers.

Bubba loved watching Lucy interact with the animals. She fed them daily and enjoyed bathing Tonka in the spring. Bubba found the jagged edges of a palm-tree branch made an excellent brush for Tonka and Cocoa, and to his surprise she brushed her own hair before brushing the animals. The animals became very fond of Lucy and looked forward to their daily brushings. One day Bubba looked up from his chores and saw Lucy riding Cocoa along the seashore. She was laughing and waving at Bubba.

Lucy normally stayed until dark and walked back to her cave after dinner. Bubba had ignored her for the most part since she had become intoxicated with wine a few weeks earlier. He prepared dinner for Lucy each night, and afterwards he would go inside his hut, leaving her alone beside the fire. He knew Lucy had to be free to make her own choices. When he lay down at night he always fell asleep with Lucy on his mind. She slept just outside his hut, and he hoped one night she would come inside by her own free will. He longed for her simple touch, and dreamed about the day he would be holding Lucy in his arms.

One night after Bubba had cooked and ate, he nodded goodnight to Lucy and walked inside his hut. He was almost asleep when he heard Lucy enter. She had brought her club with her. Bubba watched with one eye open as she lay down in the bed and fell asleep. Bubba smiled to himself. It would only be a matter of time, he thought, until she would be lying in his bed.

While fishing the following morning, Bubba found a small round shell lying in the shallow surface of the water. He picked the oyster up and opened it. Inside was a beautiful round pearl. He marveled at the pearl and thought it would make a good gift for Lucy. He returned to the hut, opening his hand, showing Lucy the pearl. Lucy took the pearl from Bubba's hand and examined it. She looked at Bubba and smiled for the first time at something he had done. She pointed at the sea suggesting more pearls.

Bubba hurried back to the sea, waded into the surf and swim toward the coral reef. The current was fast and strong, and the shells were under the coral, making them difficult to harvest. Bubba dove under the reef and gathered a basket of shells and brought them to Lucy. She watched with anticipation while he opened each shell. Bubba found only two pearls out of the many shells he opened.

He handed the pearls to Lucy. She smiled and pointed toward the sea, gesturing for more pearls. Bubba returned to the reef and by the end of the day Lucy had a handful of pearls. She pointed to the sea again. Bubba was too tired to return. When he refused to get more pearls, Lucy jumped to her feet, shouted, and threw the pearls at Bubba.

Bubba angrily stormed into the hut. He could not believe after all his hard work Lucy could react the way she had. This creature God had sent, he reasoned, was far more complicated than he had ever expected. What made Lucy happy also made her very sad, especially when there was no more. He thought Lucy to be very selfish, and thought to himself the next time she could dive for her own pearls. Bubba tried to sleep, but he was too angry. He hurried outside the hut, got on his hands and knees, and searched the sand until he had found every pearl. He walked to the surf and tossed them into the sea. Lucy saw this and cried. When Bubba saw Lucy cry, he sat down inside his hut and also cried.

Lucy wiped away her tears and yelled for Tonka. He quickly came to her side. She mounted Cocoa and rode away. When she did not return that night Bubba grew very distraught. She had taken Tonka with her, which further angered Bubba. Tonka slept inside the hut each night with Bubba, and now Tonka was also gone. Bubba found it hard to sleep and sat beside the fire all night with Gork, waiting for Lucy and Tonka to return. He thought about what he had done and felt very foolish. He felt good when he had tossed the pearls into the sea but now, he realized, it was he who was suffering.

Early the following morning, Bubba climbed the trail leading to the cliff. He knew God was always close by but also realized He was very busy with His kingdom.

Although God didn't answer, it gave Bubba great satisfaction just knowing God was listening.

After Bubba finished talking with God, he walked to the seashore and searched for the pearls. The tide had receded and Bubba was able to find many of the pearls where he had thrown them. He returned to his hut where he strung the pearls together and made a necklace for Lucy. He never wanted to make her cry again. The pearls, he thought, would bring back her smile, and it did.

Lucy and Tonka returned that afternoon. He was surprised to find her in a good mood, but he also kept in mind a woman was like the winds and could change directions at any time. But for now Bubba would relish the happy moment. Lucy dismounted Cocoa and handed Bubba a small gold nugget. She smiled and pointed toward a hill where she had found it. Bubba examined the nugget. He had never seen anything like it. He held the nugget in his hand, so overwhelmed by the gift he could hardly grunt. It was a moment he would never forget. Bubba reached into his pocket and handed Lucy the necklace. Lucy looked at Bubba with tears in her eyes. Bubba's face formed into a frown. He didn't understand why Lucy was crying when she should be happy. Lucy put her arms around Bubba's waist and gave him a brief but affectionate hug. Bubba soon realized a woman cries when she is happy or sad. He understood these tears were happy, and hoped the sad tears were gone forever.

Lucy's hug lifted Bubba to a state of giddiness he had never experienced. He felt his palms sweat and heard his heart beating like the pounding surf. He had a sick feeling in the pit of his stomach and didn't understand what was happening. It didn't matter. All Bubba wanted was to be with Lucy forever and he would never again doubt God's wisdom.

While Lucy strung the pearls around her neck, Bubba pointed to himself and said, "Bubba." Lucy repeated the word. He then gestured to Lucy and said her name, which Lucy repeated. He raised his eyes to the Heavens and said, "God." Lucy looked to the Heavens with a puzzled face. Bubba pointed to himself and then to Lucy, and back to the Heavens. Lucy did not understand something she couldn't see but still uttered the word "God" and motioned toward the Heavens. Bubba repeated the names of the animals and looked up to see Gork soaring through the skies. Bubba said, "Gork," and Lucy smiled and repeated, "Gork." The remainder of the day was spent repeating their newfound names to one another and coining a new language of their own.

Bubba lay in bed that night thinking about what a wonderful day it had been. He thought about Lucy and how things could go bad one day and good the next. He began to formulate his own philosophy of living based on his brief experience. In a short time he understood pain and pleasure and realized that pain was necessary to understand pleasure. He thought about anger and how to control it. He thought about how important forgiveness was and he was certain he had overcome most of his faults. But most of all he thought about how Lucy had put her arms around him and how good it felt.

Bubba was about to fall asleep when he heard Lucy enter the hut. He pretended to be asleep and watched with one eye open as Lucy slipped into the bed he had made for her. It was quiet inside except for the sound of the sea and the soothing voice of a gentle breeze drifting through the hut. Bubba lay wide awake. Lucy was lying on her side, turned away from Bubba. She was close enough for Bubba to hear her breathing and smell the scent of her hair, which was enough to arouse his basic animal instincts. His palms began to sweat once again and his heart pounded out of control. He could no longer control the urge to be close to Lucy. He slipped out of his cover and into Lucy's bed, and attempted to put his arms around her. Lucy awoke and sprung to her feet. She removed the club by her side and hit Bubba over the head. Bubba yelled a painful grunt and stormed out of the hut.

The moon was full, casting its light on the spring. Bubba walked a short distance to the spring and knelt on his knees, looking at his reflection, and for the first time in many years, splashed away at it. He cupped his hand full of water and poured it over his head where a lump had begun to swell. He now fully understood the word pain and quickly forgot his new philosophy on anger and forgiveness. He stood and yelled for Tonka and Cocoa. In a few moments they were by his side.

Lucy stood outside the hut and watched Bubba mount Cocoa. The club was still in her hand when Bubba approached. He stopped in front of her just long enough to give an angry grunt. He then turned and rode away without saying a word.

He rode most of the night without any particular destination. By morning he was far away from the hut. While he road along the seashore he wondered how could this thing called a woman be a nightmare but also a pleasant dream. Every time he touched the knot on the top of his head, he fumed in anger. He thought about what God had told him, and now he understood what God meant when he said "miserable at times." Bubba was also mad at himself for not controlling his anger. He realized he was reacting out of emotion and not logic.

How could he forgive a woman who had just put the third knot on his head? He needed time to be alone and figure things out. He found a peaceful spot under a tree by the sea, dismounted Cocoa and remained there in prayer for almost two days.

Lucy paced the seashore. She missed Bubba, regretted hitting him, and feared he might never return. A feeling of loneliness and guilt overwhelmed her. It was an emotion she had never experienced. She felt sick to her stomach, unsure how to deal with her guilt. She clenched her fists, kicked the sand in anger, then brought her hands to her hips and stood looking out across the ocean in deep thought. She turned and raised her eyes toward the cliff. Bubba spent a lot of time on the cliff; she thought she might find him there. She walked to the wooden trail and began her ascent to the top. When she reached the summit she was out of breath, and stopped for a moment to wipe the sweat from her face before focusing on her surroundings. Her face turned into a disappointing frown when she saw Bubba was not on the cliff. She walked to the large rock and looked out at the sea with her eyes full of tears.

While she cried, the beautiful light of God appeared and suddenly overwhelmed her. Struggling off the rock Lucy fell to the ground, lifting her eyes upward to the light.

"I am the living God, Lucy, the one who created you. Hear my words and henceforth you will understand. Go forth and serve the man I have given you, and he shall serve you. A woman is the rock upon which a man stands and without a rock man would perish, for only a woman can give life, and it is because of a good woman that man does good deeds unto my name. In my kingdom both are equal, and one could not exist without the other. You, Lucy, are the fruit of the world, and from you springs the tree of life and hope for all mankind.

"I understand, Lord," uttered Lucy.

"Weep no more, Lucy, but rejoice in my name and have a good life and many children. Bubba is a very special creature and in him I see great things to come. His work on earth has yet to begin. Now go in peace and remember I will always be with you."

When the light faded, Lucy struggled to her feet. Her knees were weak and she felt faint. She was embraced by the spirit and rejuvenated by His light and love. The words God spoke would change Lucy forever. She walked down the cliff a different woman.

Bubba began his journey home. He had prayed about his problems and came to understand his actions against Lucy were born out of his own selfish desire and needs. The bump on his head was well deserved, he reasoned, and was a good reminder to always think of another's needs and wishes before your own. His destiny, he knew, was in the will of God, and not of man. He discovered while fasting and praying, the answer to problems are only revealed when a person is ready to embrace them, surrendering to a higher power than oneself. He understood people can only grow spiritually when they learn from their mistakes.

When Bubba returned, Lucy was waiting by the seashore. She had been there all day, anticipating his return. She fully understood her purpose, and was a born-again person, filled with a passion and euphoria. The sky, the ocean, and every detail in God's creation rushed through her soul and she understood the beauty of it all.

Lucy saw Gork flying overhead, then turned and saw Bubba. She ran along the seashore, yelling his name, out of breath and pointing toward the Heavens when she reached him.

"God," she said, pointing her finger toward the Heaven.

Bubba could not believe the change in Lucy. Her eyes were full of life and her face was radiant and aglow. Bubba was certain God had spoken to her. He was overwhelmed with joy and looked into the Heavens, nodding his head in approval. He looked at Lucy with a wide grin. Lucy smiled back; her whole personality was expressed in that one happy gesture. Bubba held his hand out to Lucy. Instead of taking his hand, she reached down and picked up a seashell and placed it in his palm.

She stood, smiling at Bubba. Her face was so radiant the sun seemed to shine through her eyes. Lucy took Bubba's hand and they walked along the beach toward home.

* * * * *

Bubba and Lucy developed a close friendship over the following weeks, quickly creating a language of their own and communicating with ease. They prayed together daily and realized through prayer they had a divine mission. They often prayed about their destiny but learned God would reveal their purpose when He was ready. They turned their attention to developing a strong bond between themselves, and everything they did together was done in the glory of God.

Humor and laughter were very important to Bubba.

He never forgot what God had told him, "Laughter is good medicine for the heart and the soul." Bubba often imitated the animals in the forest as Lucy tried to guess which animal he was mimicking. Bubba invented games with sticks and stones that they played before dinner. He loved to draw funny faces in the sand that would make Lucy laugh, and soon she was drawing for him.

One afternoon Lucy was stung by a jellyfish and ran, crying, to Bubba, throwing her arms around him. It was the first time she had ever held him close. She cried in Bubba's arms until he reluctantly broke the embrace to doctor her foot. The moment was one Bubba would never forget. It was the first time she showed total dependence on his help.

A full season had passed since God had spoken to Lucy. The skies were beginning to show signs of winter, and the chilly nights had arrived. Bubba had not thought a lot about romance and had become accustomed to sleeping alone at nights and away from Lucy's snoring that often kept him awake. A time of celibacy had given them the opportunity to bond far beyond a sexual relationship. They had become perfectly united spiritually and had formed a deep friendship and respect for one another far beyond their primal instincts.

One winter night Bubba awoke and found Lucy curled up beside him. He smiled to himself and nudged her closer, slipping his arm around her. She rested her head on his shoulder. He slipped his arms around her and felt her breath against his neck, and for the first time her snores didn't bother him but sounded like sweet music to his ears.

The following spring Lucy's stomach began to swell. A woman's intuition told her she was having a child. Bubba's excitement was hard to contain. Neither Bubba nor Lucy knew anything about the birth process and they could only guess how long the little creature would remain inside her womb. They wondered if the child would be a male or a female, and Bubba prayed the child would have many fingers and toes and would favor Lucy and not him. The very idea of producing an offspring was overwhelming. They could only attribute this tiny miracle to God, and prayed daily for God to watch over their baby and show them what to do when the time arrived.

Bubba made plans for a new home. He stood with Lucy on the spot where he decided to build, raising his finger to the sky and drawing Lucy an outline. He wanted a big home with many rooms for a large family. The house would be up on the hill, below the cliff and close to the river. Bubba explained to Lucy it would take many seasons to build and would require a lot of hard work. Lucy was very excited about having a real home and wanted to help Bubba build it.

While the two waited for the child to arrive, Bubba began work on the home. He made brick out of water and clay, and cut and shaped timbers for the foundation and the roof. He designed the house on the sand using a stick to show Lucy where the fireplace, kitchen, and other rooms would be located.

Lucy worked alongside Bubba on the riverbank where they mixed clay and made bricks. Bubba kept a constant eye on Lucy. He made sure she wasn't overworked and got plenty of rest. At night Bubba put his ear to Lucy's stomach, hoping the child would at least grunt or belch so Bubba would know the child was alive. Then one day, Bubba felt Lucy's womb move. The fetus gave a small kick. Bubba jumped for joy. The idea he and Lucy could create another life was hard for him to imagine. He was constantly baffled by the birth process and soon stopped trying to understand it.

By the end of the following winter, Lucy swelled so big she could hardly walk and spent most days in bed. Bubba stopped work on the home and remained by her side. A few weeks later, on a hot summer night, Bubba awoke when he heard Lucy scream. She screamed again, loud enough to awaken Tonka and bring him to his feet. Lucy turned her head and painfully nodded to Bubba, indicating the time had arrived. She gripped his hand with all her strength and labored until early morning. Bubba sat helplessly beside her, wishing he could do more than just hold her hand.

As the night slowly gave birth to a waiting sun, it was done on earth as it was in Heaven and the cry of a newborn baby was heard louder than Bubba could ever imagine. God instructed Bubba what to do, but Bubba was not aware God had a hand in the delivery.

Bubba held up the baby girl and proudly showed it to Lucy, who gave a painful smile and cried out again. In a few moments, the cry of another baby filled Heaven and earth. Bubba's mouth dropped open and his eyes grew wide as he now beheld another little creature, a baby boy. Bubba cradled the boy and girl in his arms and showed Lucy. He was now the proud father of beautiful twins with more fingers and toes than he could count.

When God had rested He awoke on the tenth day, and He was happy He had created twins.

When He saw what He had done He was very proud and went about His business.

They named the boy Zi, after the rising sun, and named the girl Zia, after the setting sun. The birth of Zi and Zia elevated Bubba and Lucy to a new dimension, a new joy, and a love they never knew existed. They loved and adored the twins, who looked just alike but had separate personalities. On the day they were born, Bubba took them onto the cliff and held them up toward the Heavens to show God what he had created and to give thanks.

The twins had just turned two years old when Bubba laid the last brick on his home. He built the fireplaces out of colorful stones gathered from the riverbed and shaped beautiful redwood pillars and beams to support the house. He was especially proud of the floors. He had never walked on anything but the earth, and now he walked on hard oak wood he had meticulously chopped into boards to make a floor. Lucy weaved straw mats for each room and created artwork out of clay and seashells.

The cooking area was the pride of the home. It had two raised fireplaces for cooking, large pantries and a huge window with a view of the river. To the south lay the main entrance and the dining room which hosted a large oak dining table and view of the sea. The four bedrooms were located in the rear of the house. In the back yard Bubba built a barn where he fed the animals, which now included goats, rabbits, and pigs he had caught in the wild and bred.

Bubba was proud of the house and the farm he had created with his own two hands. He named his property Kismira, which in his own language meant "holy ground." On Kismira there was always plenty of work to be done, and soon Bubba would have plenty of help.

In the next five years, Lucy gave birth to three more children. Their next-born was a girl they named Makia, after the earth, then Celeste, after the moon, and last, a boy they named Michael after the angels in Heaven.

Bubba and Lucy were quick to realize that all their children were very different, and they loved all of them equally. Celeste was soft-spoken and seldom showed her emotions. She liked to cook and help tend the garden. Makia was appropriately named after the earth. She was a happy child who liked to dabble in clay and make jewelry out of stones and seashells, while Michael was more shy and timid. Unlike his older brother, Zi, who was a natural-born warrior and leader, Michael was a thinker and never accepted anything as fact until he reasoned it out.

Bubba and Lucy tried to spend equal time with each child. When the children were old enough to understand spiritual matters, Bubba and Lucy spoke to them about God, and how God had created the two of them for one another. Bubba told his children about his days in the dark forest and how he was saved by God while crossing the great sea. Each morning Bubba took his children to the cliff, where he taught them how to pray and worship

God. He spoke about the many sacred covenants God had given him and tried to instill those traits in his children.

"We are family," he told the children at an early age. "Our bonds of love and friendship must never be broken. We must all love one another and work together for the good of everyone. No one person is more important than the other, and none of us is more important than God."

Bubba's teachings would form a friendship and a bond between the children that would never be broken in the years to come.

The children grew up with Tonka, Gork and Cocoa as their only friends outside the family. They loved riding Cocoa and playing with Tonka. The children explored the many caves in the countryside but were only allowed to wander off Kismira with Tonka by their side and with Gork as their guide home.

Bubba built a boat for his family, just large enough for everyone to fit comfortably inside. It took a full year to build. It was crude, with a wooden rudder and a sail made of animal hides, but his efforts proved worthy of the hard labor. The children loved the boat for more reasons than one. It gave them a way to escape Kismira. They enjoyed sailing, and the boat gave them a freedom away from the ears and eyes of their parents. Zi and Zia learned to navigate the river with their younger brothers and sisters, and it was on the river the siblings forged their strongest bonds. They fished, crabbed and looked for turtle eggs together. They discussed their solitary existence, talked about their future and questioned the existence of the God about whom their parents talked. Although they respected their parents, they found it hard to believe in something they could not see or touch. The children could only believe in reality as they experienced it, and to believe in anything intangible made no sense to them.

Just off the inlet was a small group of islands rising out of the sea . . . small mountains that dotted along the horizon a few miles away. During the summer months, Bubba took his family to the islands to fish and to enjoy the lazy summer afternoons. The children named their favorite island, "Bali," meaning high. At the top, Bali towered a hundred feet, high enough for the children to climb to the top and dive into a pool of water beneath a huge waterfall. Bubba and Lucy normally found a comfortable spot to rest while they watched their children dive from the rocks and play together under the waterfall. Bali was a majestic island, small enough to walk around its perimeter within an hour and a short climb to its highest peak.

The children respected and loved their parents but as they grew older even Bali became boring and they began to confront their parents. They wanted to know if they were doomed to spend their lives isolated on a seashore and if others like themselves existed, and questioned when they too would be married and have children. Zi respected his father's beliefs but thought him a little bit on the crazy side for worshiping a God he couldn't see. Michael was quick to agree, citing that their father had proof of nothing other than a good imagination. They wanted a reasonable explanation about where their parents had come from. The concept of an unseen God and parents without parents was something they found hard to comprehend, much less accept.

Both Zi and Zia were close to thirteen years of age and had become very discontented with their solitary existence. Zi was as tall as his father and had become a handsome young man with long dark hair and blue eyes.

Zia too was tall and as beautiful as her mother. Her long dark hair flowed down to her waist and she had sparkling blue eyes just like her brother. She was approaching womanhood and worried about her future. Zi and Zia often talked about leaving home, in search of other creatures like themselves, but Bubba was quick to dismiss any such notion.

Before the twins' next birthday, something totally unexpected happened that would forever change their destiny. A young handsome stranger with long golden hair appeared on horseback. He was dressed in colorful garments and wore a plate of silver on his chest. Across his back was strung a bow and arrow, and on his side he wore a silver sword. It was the younger children, Makia and Celeste, who first spotted the stranger near the sea, trotting along on a huge black animal they had never seen. They were out of breath, having run from the seashore when they reached their mother and attempted to explain what they had seen. Before Lucy could order the children inside, she lifted her eyes and saw the stranger herself. The horse snarled, and reared up on its hind legs. The rider kicked the horse with his heel, and galloped toward Bubba's homestead. Lucy and her children quickly ran inside.

Bubba and his sons stood with spears in their hands as the stranger approached and dismounted. The stranger drew the silver sword with a golden handle from his side. Bubba and his sons quickly raised their weapons. The stranger walked to Bubba, knelt on one knee and presented it to Bubba as a peace offering. Bubba was speechless. He examined the sword and handed it to Zi for inspection. Zi looked at the sword as the stranger stood and spoke. He said his name was Calio, a warrior from the Canite tribe who had been sent by his King to find the great sea that was written in the sacred scrolls of the Canite people. The tribe, he explained, was tired of war with neighboring tribes and was looking for a place to live in peace. He said his escorts had been killed along the way by bandits; he was the lone survivor.

Bubba was surprised Calio spoke in their language and wondered how it was possible when they had created their own words. He later attributed his language to the work of God. Calio was suspicious of the family who spoke his language and could give no satisfactory answer to their origins, only that they had descended from God.

Bubba invited Calio to stay for the night. Lucy prepared a feast of baked clams, oysters, and roasted deer. Over dinner the children listened in awe as Calio spoke of things of which they had never heard, and their excitement was hard to contain. He talked about war with the Adamites, a tribe that has settled in a place called Mesopotamia. He explained the Adamites claimed to be the direct descendants from a couple named Adam and Eve, who claimed they were sent by the God to bring peace and love into the world. Their mission had somehow failed, he explained, and war was the end result. He pointed in the direction of the great sea, "That is where the Canites shall soon live. Thousands will come and soon laughter and gaiety shall be heard across the mountains and valleys and war will be no more."

When he had spoken way into the night, Bubba ordered the children to bed. They could hardly sleep that night. At last, the children's dreams had come true. Calio's arrival had given them hope for a future, and their excitement was hard to contain.

Zia told her twin brother, "Yes, my brother, I will

have a handsome warrior like Calio and children beautiful as me, Zia, the setting sun."

Zi laughed, "And I, Zia, will have many wives like Calio. A wife for each season to fulfill my every wish."

Calio told Bubba he would be leaving the following morning. Bubba was pleased by the announcement. Calio had spoken of many wives and Gods. He had talked about great wealth and riches and had showed the family silver and gold coins, explaining that the coins determined a person's wealth, and how they were traded for good and services. Bubba was very suspicious of Calio and doubted what he had seen and heard.

The following morning, Bubba awoke to find Calio showing his horse to Zia. Soon the two were galloping down the beach on horseback. Bubba stood and watched. His lips formed an angry curl. Lucy approached and put a reassuring hand on Bubba. "I have never seen her so happy and laughing aloud. She is but a child, so let her be a child."

When they returned, Calio offered to take Lucy for a ride. Bubba was quick to object. Lucy obeyed Bubba's wishes and laughed, "I've always wondered if you would be jealous if another came along. It is only you I will forever love."

Calio stayed that night and two more nights thereafter. He made himself at home, acting as though he owned it through actions such as sitting down for dinner without asking permission. He paid most of his attention to Lucy, often pulling her aside and talking. This didn't go unnoticed by Bubba.

When Calio spoke about leaving in the fall, Bubba became angry. The children were intrigued by Calio's stories, but Bubba had heard enough. He told Calio it was time to leave. Calio thanked Bubba for his generosity and agreed to leave the following morning.

That night, Bubba awoke to find Lucy missing. It was still dark, just before daybreak. After a quick search of the house, he awoke Tonka from his sleep. Tonka lazily came to his feet and shook his mane. He raised his eyes at Bubba, waiting on a command.

Bubba took the sword Calio had given him and left to search for Lucy. Tonka followed close behind, still sleepy but alert and aware that trouble was on the horizon. Outside, Calio's horse was gone. Bubba pointed toward the ground, showing Tonka where the horse had stood. Tonka put his nose to the ground and sniffed. He growled and raised his eyes at Bubba. Bubba gave a nod for Tonka to follow the scent. Tonka roared with an angry growl and dashed into the woods with Bubba running close behind.

Deep into the woods, Bubba heard Lucy's frantic cry. In a few moments Bubba found Calio and Lucy in a wooden path leading along the seashore. Calio was strapping Lucy to his horse while she screamed and kicked. Her dress was torn and her face badly bruised. Calio quickly turned when he saw Bubba.

Tonka stood, his mane standing high, his hind legs ready to jump and attack on Bubba's command. Overhead the moon was slowly being replaced by the sun but the light was just enough to cast a shadow across Lucy's face. She lay strapped across the horse, breathing hard, her eyes filled with fear. Calio's expression showed surprised at the sight of Bubba. He looked at Bubba with apologetic eyes and spread his arms in a friendly gesture. Bubba's eyes shifted to Lucy. She gave a warning look to Bubba as Calio reached behind his back and removed a dagger. Before Calio had a chance to throw the knife,

Bubba raised the sword hidden by his side and thrust it into Calio's heart. Calio fell to the ground, first on his knees and then backwards. He lay on the ground with the sword stuck in his chest. Bubba looked at Lucy and back on Calio's body. He was speechless and couldn't believe he had killed a man.

Bubba walked to Calio and planted his foot on his chest. He slid the sword from Calio's heart, then turned and looked at Lucy. Her face was pale. She was too weak to stand on her own. Bubba dropped the sword at his feet and walked to Lucy and took her into his arms. He then carried her home without a word being spoken.

The children were asleep. Bubba put Lucy quietly to bed and returned to the spot where he had killed Calio. He stood over the dead man and looked down at his face, taking a deep breath and wiping the sweat from his own forehead. He was breathing hard, perspiring so profusely the sweat burned his eyes, blurring his vision. He wiped his eyes and squatted next to Calio because his knees were weak. He brought his hands together, cupping them, trembling and trying to figure out what he should do. Calio lay with his mouth slightly parted and his eyes wide open, with the same surprised expression he had had when Bubba thrust the sword through his heart. Bubba found it hard to look at Calio's face. He covered it with a bush and began digging a hole with his hands. When the grave was deep enough, he rolled Calio's body over and watched it tumble into the hole.

After burying Calio, he stood and looked at Calio's horse. He stroked the horse gently and looked at Tonka, who was resting on all fours and watching. The horse reared his head and rolled his eyes at Bubba. Bubba knew he needed to kill the horse and bury it. He feared others would look for Calio and find his horse. He picked his sword up and drew back at the horse to slash it across the neck, but slowly lowered the sword. The horse had done no harm, he thought. He untied the horse and motioned for Tonka to chase it away, and Tonka obliged. Bubba hoped the horse would never return; it didn't.

It was midmorning when Bubba emerged from the woods and walked to the seashore. He dropped to his knees at the edge of the surf and washed the blood and dirt off his body. He was beginning to feel the full impact of what he had done and was consumed with guilt. A man was dead, and he didn't know what to tell his children: the truth or a lie. He searched his heart for answers but couldn't find a satisfactory solution. He had always taught the truth but now concluded he had to instruct Lucy to tell the children Calio had left for his homeland and to ask her never to mention the incident.

In just a few days after meeting his first person outside the family, he had expressed anger, jealously, mistrust, committed murder and lied to his children.

After he washed the blood from his hands, he walked to the cliff and spent the night and the following morning in prayer and meditation. He understood he could find the answers within himself if he truly let his mind and heart unite with his spirit. It was like fine tuning an instrument. The music of the heart would come into play with the mind, and the voice of God could be heard when everything was in harmony.

When he was satisfied he was forgiven, he returned home, but only with the lingering thought the murder of Calio would eventually come back to haunt him, and it did.

Bubba prepared for what he was sure to come. He knew one day the Canites would arrive as Calio had predicted and constructed a wall around his home and a watchtower overlooking the sea. He was satisfied God had forgiven him for killing Calio, and he hoped he would never have to raise an unfriendly hand against another human being.

He constructed a cellar below the house where he forged weapons and taught Zi and Michael how to defend themselves. It was there he realized Zi had the makings of a superior warrior. Zi showed his father new ways to make arrowheads, bows, and other weapons, and practiced self-defense. Michael had little interest in direct warfare or self defense but found his expertise in more subtle forms of defense such as designing the home with trap doors, fake walls and an escape tunnel in case of attack.

This was a special time for Bubba, working side by side with his sons. Zi and Michael were totally different but very smart, each in his own way. Zi used the direct approach, while Michael chose more indirect way of dealing with a hostile situation.

Zi told Michael in the cellar one day, the best way to

kill a snake was to cut off its head. Bubba agreed but Michael turned and said, "Never kill the snake when you can use it to your advantage. Its venom should be saved to make deadly wine for our enemies."

Lucy also worked side by side with her daughters while Bubba was busy with his sons. Zia was quick to learn the arts of weaving and making pottery but grew bored with anything once she had mastered it. She was more refined than her sisters, and better at giving orders than taking them. Her days were spent dreaming about the day the Canites would arrive and she could meet a man like Calio. Makia and Celeste were innovative in their own ways. Celeste loved to cook and to grow vegetables in the garden. She was a homemaker, shy and content who kept close to her mother's side. Makia was more outgoing and independent. She discovered how to make colors and stains from fruits and berries and soon became the family artist.

The women spent their afternoons making clothes together out of the many furs and animal pelts the men brought home. They didn't consider it work but a way of enjoying their summer days and often worked late into the night competing with one another for the best design.

* * * * *

A few months after Calio was killed, Lucy announced she was with child. Everyone was overjoyed but very surprised. Lucy had told her family she couldn't have any more children. It had been more than twelve years since the birth of her last child, Michael, and she was fast approaching the age of forty. She and Bubba had attempted to have more children but were unsuccessful.

The following spring Lucy gave birth to a baby girl. Zia, Makia and Celeste helped their mother deliver the baby while the men waited anxiously just outside the room. When they heard the cry of the newborn baby, Bubba rose to his feet and laughed aloud, putting his arms around Zi and Michael. When Zia walked into the room with the baby cradled in her arms, Tonka came to his feet and growled. Gork flipped his sleepy eyes open and fluttered his wings.

The following morning, Lucy lay in bed, too weak to move. Bubba wrapped the baby in a blanket and carried her to the cliff. The children followed their father and watched him hold their sister up to the Heavens and give thanks to God for the new baby. When he had finished giving thanks, the children discussed what they should name her. They finally agreed her proper name would be Anastasia after the "water of life," but they would call her Anna. She was the first born with blond hair and green eyes, which made her exceptionally special.

The children adored their little sister and she quickly became the pride of the family. They were all old enough to appreciate the new addition and often bickered over who was the next to hold her. The family gathered in the kitchen after dinner when Anna stood for the first time, putting one foot in front of another and taking her first steps. Lucy stretched her arms open as Anna struggled to walk. When she reached her mother, Anna turned and looked at her brothers and sisters, smiled and burped. Everyone laughed and applauded. Zia quickly picked up Anna and held her close, stating, "She is mine and no one else can have her."

Makia stood and took Anna out of Zia's arms. "You can have her later. Tonight my baby sister sleeps with me."

Bubba stood and took Anna away from Makia, laid

Anna across his shoulder and gently patted her naked butt. "I am the father," he laughed. "It is my time to hold her. God has given us this beautiful child and tonight she sleeps with her mother and me."

When Anna was five years old, tragedy befell the family. She and Makia were gathering sand dollars and shells on the seashore while Tonka lay nearby, basking in the summer sun. Makia was thirteen years old. She had taken her eyes off Anna for only a short time. After she gathered a basket of shells she stood and turned to find Anna missing. She then heard Anna's cry for help. Anna had strayed too far out into the surf and was swept away by a strong undercurrent. Anna had learned to swim by the age of three but the currents were too strong. Makia stood helplessly and watched her sister drift further out to sea.

Makia's screams for help reached the family. Bubba and Lucy were tending the garden when they looked up and saw Anna fighting the deadly currents. Bubba rushed to the seashore and jumped into the water with Tonka by his side. Anna had drifted outside the coral reef that buffeted the beach where the currents were strong and fast.

It was late afternoon. A heavy blanket of fog had settled just above the sea. Bubba swam to the reef, his eyes searching the dense fog for Anna. Tonka continued swimming beyond the reef. Bubba heard Anna's cry but couldn't see her. The tide was too swift for Bubba to swim any further. He could only stand on the reef in horror and listen as Anna's cry grew fainter the further out to sea she drifted. The fog partially cleared, and there was no sign of Tonka or Anna. Lucy and the children stood on the seashore in disbelief they were gone. In just a few minutes their lives had turned from happiness to horror . . . and their grief was just beginning.

Bubba retreated to the cliff to mourn in private. He knew prayer could not bring her back, and he searched his heart for any solution to end his grief. God had once saved Tonka and him from the sea, and he questioned why He didn't save Anna and Tonka.

Makia cried constantly, blaming herself for the tragedy by not watching Anna more closely. Her constant tears only added to the family's suffering. They were so saddened by the loss, they hardly spoke to one another for weeks.

Bubba realized he needed to do something to bring his family back together. He instructed Makia to make two wreaths, one for Anna and the other one for Tonka. Makia walked to the woods and gathered branches. While she was breaking twigs from the trees, she looked up to find Celeste had followed her into the forest. Soon Michael was standing behind Celeste and offering to help, followed by Zi and Zia, who came when they saw their brothers and sisters helping Makia. While the children gathered twigs, Zia was the first to break the silence. She walked to Makia, and put a flower into her basket. "I know that you think you are to blame. I hear your cries at night. If you are to blame then we are all to blame for not being with you."

The children gathered around Makia. Celeste took her sister's hand in hers. "We do not blame you for our sister's death. There is nothing you could have done to save her. We are all family, and together we shall see ourselves through this."

Makia burst into tears. The children circled around Makia with reassuring hands and held their sister until she stopped crying. The final tears would be a temporary closure for Makia. Her nightmares were just beginning. After regaining her composure, she wiped the last tear from her eye. She smiled at her brothers and sisters with a look of relief and sent Zi and Zia to the seashore to gather shells. She instructed Michael and Celeste to gather the most beautiful flowers they could find.

When Bubba and Lucy saw the children talking to one another and making the wreath, they were very pleased. At sunset Bubba took his family to the seashore. He and Lucy watched as the children tossed flowers into the sea. Bubba gathered his family into a circle, and said a prayer while they joined hands. Zi and Zia handed the two wreaths to their parents. Bubba and Lucy tossed the wreaths into the surf and watched them drift out to sea. Then, one by one, the children returned back to home with not a word spoken, leaving their parents by themselves on the seashore. Bubba prayed for God's guidance, and his prayers were answered. The ceremony brought the family back together, but the loss of Anna and Tonka would always be a memory they would never erase.

The following summer the earth roared like thunder from the sound of the Canites arriving. The family gathered in the watchtower and watched in awe as caravan after caravan with hundreds of horses, mules, and camels slowly made their way across the hills and filled the countryside just across the river. The spectacular sight lasted all day. When darkness arrived, the country looked like a thousand sparkling stars from the many campfires that lit up the river.

The next morning, Bubba secured his home and forbade anyone outside the walls. He hoped they had come in peace. There were far too many for him and his two sons to fight, so they watched and waited.

By noon the following day a warrior on horseback crossed the river. He had three camels in tow behind him. When he reached the gates to Bubba's home, the warrior spoke.

"My name is Dante," he said, "son of the great King Caligastia. We come in peace and my father sends his blessings."

Dante then motioned for the servants to unload three large boxes stacked on the camels. "These are gifts from the king. He invites you and your family to join the

Canites in our celebration of freedom from the Adamites. May we enter your home?"

Inside, the servants displayed an array of fine jewelry, furs, gold and silver coins, coffee, and other items. To Bubba, Dante brought back the memory of Calio, who had also come as a friend and betrayed them. Bubba had instructed his children the day the Canites arrived, they were never to mention the name Calio. The children gave each other suspicious glances at the odd request but obeyed their father's wishes. Bubba feared the new neighbors might be the tribe Calio had spoken about, and they were.

Dante was young, handsome, and especially charming. His long black hair curled and dropped on his shoulders. Tall, lean, and muscular, he looked like a person to be feared at first glance, but his commanding presence was quickly disarmed by his gentle eyes and wide smile.

Bubba introduced Dante first to Lucy and then to his children, calling each one by name. When he had finished, Dante's eyes stayed fixed on Zia. It was obvious to the others Dante was entranced by Zia's beauty. Dante's thoughts were interrupted by a loud grunt from Bubba. Lucy covered her mouth to hide her laugh. Zia blushed. Makia and Celeste giggled.

Dante quickly diverted his eyes, and looked at Bubba. He bowed his head in apology. "She is very beautiful." Turning his eyes his eyes at Lucy, he added, "As beautiful as her mother."

Bubba looked at Dante with a suspicious eye. The look told Dante it was time to leave. He bowed graciously to the family and kissed Lucy on her hand while keeping one eye on Zia. Bubba took a step toward Dante as he kissed Lucy's hand. He looked at Dante with a puzzled expression and groaned under his breath. The children giggled at their father's behavior. Dante nodded a goodbye at the family and quickly left.

The children gathered around their father, begging him to accept Dante's invitation. Bubba reluctantly agreed, but only after he had talked it over with Lucy. He remembered how Calio had come as a friend and later deceived the family. He was also suspicious of the man who had just kissed Lucy's hand. It was a custom he didn't like. He thought the next time he saw Dante he would kiss his hand and see if he liked it. Nevertheless, Bubba agreed to go for the sake of the family. He knew it was important to make friends with his new neighbors.

The following week Dante arrived with two of the king's finest carriages to escort Bubba and his family to the celebration. A team of the king's beautiful Arabian horses pulled the carriages. No one was surprised when Dante took Zia's hand and helped her into the lead carriage, while Bubba and his family were seated in the second one. It was hard for the children to contain their excitement. They were embarking on a journey into a new world. The children often joked to their parents they were sick of looking at one another. Now there would be hundreds of other people to see and with whom to talk.

Makia best described the trip to her mother as the carriage crossed the river. "Mother," she said with a jest, "your children have finally been let out of their cage."

* * * * *

King Caligastia was a big, burly man with a crop of silver hair and a thick white beard. He was an imposing figure with his long white robe accented by the solid gold jewelry draped around his neck. On each finger was a gold-and-diamond ring, and both his wrist were covered with numerous diamond-studded bracelets. Many wives and servants stood by to obey his every wish.

Dante had earlier explained to Bubba his family had ruled over the Canites for a little over two hundred years and his father was the eighth successor to the throne, claiming a heritage and bloodline directly from the gods during the days of an evil man named Lucifer.

Arriving at the celebration, Bubba and his family were treated like royalty. They had assigned seats at the king's table and each family member had a personal server. The king had previously referred to them as mere peasants, but at Dante's urging the king agreed to the special treatment, citing this was a celebration, a time for wine, song, and dance.

The celebration, dress, and the people were a cultural shock for the family. They marveled at the lavish display of lamb, ox, and other dishes they had never tasted. They drank wine from solid silver cups and sat quietly in awe of the hundreds of people inside a canvas tent three times the size of their own home. Lucy and her daughters couldn't believe the colorful clothes, the wardrobes, shoes, and dyed hair. They whispered to one another, pointing at the painted faces of the women and their unique jewelry.

Before dinner, the king stood and clapped his hands. The room fell silent from the chatter and noise of the crowd. He spoke briefly to the people, holding a cup high while the crowd applauded.

When the king sat down, the festivities began. Dancers dressed as different gods paraded in front of the king to the music of drums, horns, and other instruments. A play was staged, symbolizing the Canite's victory over the Adamites, and later, women dressed in thin silk barely covering their bodies danced the better part of the night.

Zia was seated beside Dante and away from the family. She had spent all day preparing for the dinner, and wore a simple but elegant dress made from finely woven lamb's wool and a necklace made from small colorful stones. Her face was free of makeup, and the fresh look set her apart from other Canite women. Dante was totally intrigued by her beauty. Her smile was contagious, and her personality and poise quickly won his heart.

Zia was just as infatuated with Dante. He was a handsome warrior, and underneath the tough exterior Zia found him warm and charming. The most attractive thing about him, she thought, was his sense of humor. He kept her laughing most of the night and she found herself in a world she had always dreamed about.

Zi was seated with Fabia. She had just turned eighteen and was petite, with long pitch-black hair woven into dreadlocks. She wore a thin gold headband with matching gold necklaces and bracelets. Her dark green eyes, olive skin, and long silk dress gave her a stunning appearance. Many of the guests commented they made an attractive couple.

But it was the twins who made the greatest impression with the guests. The Canites had never seen twins, and their height, their poise and friendly dispositions won the hearts of everyone that had a chance to meet them.

After dinner, when Dante had introduced Zia to many of his friends, he asked her to walk outside for a breath of night air. They left the dinner party and stopped just outside the tent.

"I am pleased you are here," said Dante.

"I have looked forward to the occasion since the invitation," Zia responded.

"Will I see you again?"

"Time will tell," responded Zia. "I am a very busy person. I have goats to milk and animals to feed."

"And you, Zia, I am certain, don't know a goat from a sheep. I could never imagine you milking a goat."

"But you believed me if only for a moment, didn't you?"

"Yes, but never again. You only avoided my question."

"Then I will be totally honest with you, Dante. Is that your wish? "

"Yes, Zia. Always be honest with me."

"Then the answer is yes, I do know the difference between a goat and a sheep."

Dante burst into laughter. "You, Zia, have done it to me again."

Zia joked, "You told me to be honest."

"I like a woman who can make me laugh. You are very refreshing to be with. I have a carriage a short walk away. Would you like for me to show you around?"

Zia, laughed, and said, "As my father always says, why not?"

* * * * *

Bubba and Lucy had seen enough of the Canite way of life. They were glad they had come but now were ready to leave. They agreed with one another the best part of the evening was the dinner. The food was delicious but they cared little for the noisy chatter, the music, the nudity, and the talk of many gods and wives. Bubba furthermore didn't like the effects the wine had on the guests. Everyone at the celebration looked intoxicated.

Although he had earlier forbidden his children to drink the wine, they had. It was the first time they had ever disobeyed their father. And Bubba cared little for the king. He found him loud and obnoxious. The remnants of the king's dinner dangled in his beard for most of the evening, painting a poor picture of so called royalty to Bubba.

The king had not spoken directly to Bubba and Lucy the entire night but often glanced in their direction while talking. He was drunk and self-centered. After dinner he looked directly at Bubba and Lucy for the first time and boasted, "I have more children than I can count, twenty-seven if I remember correctly. But many claim I am their father." He laughed in self amusement. "But I only lay claim to children by my first wife, my two spoiled children, Fabia and Dante."

One of the king's wives leaned over and whispered in his ear. The king nodded to his wife and raised a finger. "Ah, yes, there is another missing I also claim. His name is Calio, my oldest."

The king now had Bubba's and Lucy's attention. They stopped eating and turned their eyes at the king, listening to his every word.

The king lowered his eyes, momentarily lost in thought. He then raised his eyes at Bubba and Lucy and, strangely, directed the comment to them. "But he was murdered by bandits while searching for the lost sea which we have now found."

The king turned his eyes toward the others and lifted his cup, "But tonight we will not dwell on the past but think of the future."

Bubba and Lucy were speechless. They felt the blood drain from their faces, paling their complexions. They dared not look at one another because they knew what the other was thinking. The fact that the king looked directly at them when he made the comment sent chills down their spines. Perhaps it was just a coincidence, but nevertheless it was unnerving. They prayed the name Calio would never be said again. The awful memories of that night flooded their thoughts like an unwelcome tide rushing in unexpectedly. They were ready to leave the celebration.

Bubba and Lucy turned in their chairs. They looked for Zia but did not see her. They motioned for Zi, who was soon standing beside them. He informed his parents Zia had left with Dante for a carriage ride, but not to worry. Lucy motioned for Michael, Makia, and Celeste, pointing toward the entrance. They were seated at the end of the table and gave a disappointed look. Lucy knew they wanted to stay. They were obviously enjoying the celebration but respected their mother's wishes and rose from their seats. Bubba thanked the king for his hospitality. The king made no comment but only snapped his fingers for a servant to bring the carriages to the front of the tent. He was glad the family was leaving. Bubba noticed the king observing his fingers and toes, perhaps wondering how such a man could have such a beautiful wife and attractive family.

Bubba and Lucy said little to one another on the ride home. They were escorted in the lead carriage while the children rode in another carriage directly behind. The children were laughing and singing as the carriage crossed the shallow part of the river. The parents were happy the children had had a good time. It would be a night talked about among the family for a long time, but for now Bubba and Lucy could only sit in silence and think about what the king had said. *Calio!*

They looked out across the mouth of the sea where a half-moon hung above the horizon. The sea and the river would always remain special to them. They had first met at the spring with the sea at their doorstep and the river beside them. It was there they had raised their children and had spent the best days of their lives.

Now a different wind drifted across the waters; an unfamiliar breeze crept across the sea and stirred their souls and unsettled their minds. Most of their days on Kismira had been happy, filled with laughter and gaiety. But now they heard thunder in their hearts and felt storms slowly brewing within themselves. They felt fear for the first time in many years and found it hard to embrace.

The twins were old enough to remember Calio very well, and Bubba and Lucy feared it just a matter of time until the name of Calio was mentioned in their presence. Should they tell the children what happened? Then what should they do? Ask them to lie about it? How would they answer for his death? Should they go to the king and confess to the truth or should they remain silent? They had served God with all their hearts and now found themselves living a lie with no immediate absolution , only fear and indecision.

Bubba realized truth could not be suppressed for any length of time. Truth, he was certain, would always prevail, surface, emerge, manifest, and reveal itself. Somehow, somewhere, sooner or later it would triumph. He had taught his children they could run but they could not hide; that the past will always be part of the future; it was important to confront the past if need be, before it confronted them.

Now Bubba's own words had come back to haunt

him. It was a dilemma, a crisis of the heart for which he had no answers, and he knew truth had time on its side. It was like a serpent, waiting patiently to strike, and Bubba knew one day the truth would surface. But little did Bubba know the painful sacrifice that would be made for the murder of Calio when the serpent did strike.

* * * * *

Dante and Zia sat in the grass on a cliff high above the sea. They watched the village campfires below twinkling in the misty dark and heard the music of the ongoing celebration carried across the valley by the ocean wind.

It had been a steep-but-fun climb. It was the first time Zia had actually been with a man outside the family. She enjoyed every touch of Dante's hand — gripping hers, holding her arm, and feeling herself being lifted up by Dante aroused her more intimate thoughts. She had dreamed about romance and the realization was unfolding with every word Dante spoke.

Dante had brought a pouch full of wine and two cups. The sun was just beginning to show its face between clouds and the two watched the fog drift slowly over the whitecaps of the sea. While Zia sipped on wine, Dante stood and pointed to a place higher up on the mountainside.

"That is where I shall build my palace one day. It will have many windows to look out over the sea and a balcony for each window, and below a thousand roses I will pick for you. One for each day."

Zia laughed, tipping her cup toward Dante. "It has been a wonderful night, more marvelous that I could have ever imagined. I have never laughed this much, or ever met a man like you."

Zia thought about what she had said and then lifted

her eyes at Dante and laughed, "In fact you are the only man I have been with. I mean, the only one that has ever held my hand. I have no other men by which to judge you. Perhaps there are many as charming as you."

Dante knelt down beside Zia, taking her hand in his. Zia had her face to the sea. Dante touched her cheek, gently tilting her face to his. The wind from the sea was just enough to lift her long hair away from her deep blue eyes. Her skin was white, fresh and unblemished, and her lips were naturally pink and had a slight part in the center. When she smiled a hint of two small dimples emerged below her cheeks.

"Never have I seen a face so beautiful. You have not a speck of paint or clay upon it yet it shines like the sun."

"And I have no doubt you have many women you say that to. You are the king's son and a great warrior. I have heard that you have killed many men and risked your life many times in the face of death. I am but a poor girl born into humble roots. You could have any woman in the Canite tribe, yet you want to be with me."

"That is true," replied Dante. "And as surely as the sun rises now before us, I made this climb up the hill to show you a dream I want you to be part of. Never shall I look at another woman."

Zia touched Dante's hand with her finger. She then brought her eyes and her finger to his face, touching him on his cheek and letting her finger slowly drop.

"And you, Dante, are very handsome. I can only judge you by the strange men I saw tonight at the celebration and didn't like. But my parents have taught me that outward appearances have little to do with the inner beauty of a person."

"I would like to talk to your parents again. I will

convince them I am worthy of their beautiful daughter."

"You have no one to convince but me," laughed Zia
"My parents are very different than anyone you shall eve
meet. It would be hard to convince them of anything
They judge a person by what they do, not what they say
Right now my father is wondering where I am and i
probably coming to look for me."

"I have had the most wonderful night of my life with
a beautiful woman from across the river. We have talked
and laughed all night and as the sun rises on your hear
and mine, I have not even kissed you."

"I have never been kissed," said Zia. "This should be
very interesting."

Dante stood with an outstretched hand. Zia stood and
took Dante's hand, facing him. He tilted her face to hi
and kissed her very softly on her lips.

* * * * *

Bubba had agonized over Zia for the most part of the
night while Lucy slept. When Zia had not returned home
by mid morning, he woke Lucy and told her about his
plans to go into the village to find her.

"She is with the king's son," said Lucy, stretching he
arms from her sound sleep. Surely nothing could happen
to her. She is a grown woman, not a child."

Bubba groaned, and said, "She will always be a child
to me."

Lucy responded. "Once you bonded me in rope and
only when you freed me did I return. Now you want to
stifle our daughter."

"This thing called wine is a poison that makes another
act like a jackass. Do you not remember you once wiggled
like a fish after you drank wine?"

"And do you remember, my dear husband, the lumps

on your head? It is never too late to put another if you continue with your foolish notions. We have raised our children well. That is all we can do. The rest is up to them."

Bubba knew Lucy spoke the truth. He feared the day he would lose just one of his children. That day came sooner than Bubba had expected. Zia returned late that morning in the royal carriage only to inform her father she was returning to the village for the night.

Bubba at first objected but soon succumbed to Zia's wishes at the urging of Lucy.

"Father," she said, "did you not travel many years to find our mother? And now I have only to travel across the river to find happiness."

Bubba insisted if she must go, she take Zi with her for her own safety. Zi was more than anxious to oblige. He was infatuated with Fabia, and now he had Dante's royal carriage to take him. When Bubba told Zi he would have to escort his sister to the village, Zi attempted to hide his smile and excitement.

After Bubba left, Zi jumped for joy, looked upwards and said, "Yes, I now believe in God."

Bubba and Lucy watched from their bedroom window as the royal carriage pulled to the entrance. Zi and Zia were waiting with their bags packed.

Dante was surprised Zi was going with Zia. He forced a smile and looked at Zia.

"My father has insisted that Zi, my brother come along," said Zia.

"You can bring everyone," said Dante with a laugh, although his tone said that he didn't mean it.

Dante gave a brief nod at Celeste and Makia, who were standing near the entrance and watching. They giggled and blushed. Watching their sister leave with a man sent an exciting message. They later talked about the time they would travel across the river and find a man like Dante.

Dante noticed Bubba and Lucy watching; he also took note of Michael standing in the watchtower. He waved at the parents and then turned and helped Zia into the carriage.

Lucy turned toward Bubba. "She is not gone forever, do not look so sad."

"She is indeed gone forever," replied Bubba.

"She will return one day," responded Lucy. "But that is her business, not ours. We must now gather the children for dinner while we have time to enjoy the rest of our family."

* * * * *

When the royal carriage reached the village, Dante sent word to Fabia that Zia had brought her brother, Zi. He knew his sister was fond of Zi and he hoped the two would enjoy seeing one another. He wanted to be alone with Zia and was at first disappointed her brother had tagged along. But Zi and Fabia enjoyed being together and it didn't spoil the evening for Dante, who was intent on putting all his efforts and charm on winning Zia.

The four dined in Dante's tent. He had camped near the sea, where a cool ocean breeze and the soothing roar of the waves pounding against the beach was just enough to stir romantic impulses. The only distractions were the hundreds of tents pitched nearby that stretched along the beach.

Dante had told his Canite neighbors he wished not to be disturbed, and they kept their distance. The side flaps of the tent remained opened throughout dinner and the only distraction was when Dante's camels and horses peeked into the tent and occasionally added their blessings to the dinner in their own way.

Before dinner Dante showed Zia and Zi his horses. His favorite horse was Hector. He treated the horse with love and affection, stroking it gently and rubbing its back, talking to it. He explained he had lost several horses in battle and Hector had survived against great odds.

Over wine, Dante apologized for the crude tent. He told Zia the tent was temporary and he had enough gold and silver to easily build a grand palace. Zia replied, "I do not care about power or wealth." Unfortunately he believed her.

Outside the tent, two servants prepared roasted lamb over an open fire. A servant entered the tent to fill Zia's wine glass. Zia looked at Dante and said, "There is no need for the servants to pour wine when it is I who will keep your cup filled."

Dante responded, "I have never met a woman who could keep my cup full."

Zia smiled softly with her intoxicating eyes fixed on his. "With me, Dante, your cup will never be empty."

Zi heard this and whispered in his sister's ear, "Is there something you have not told me, sister?"

Zia gently touched her brother's lips with her finger and replied, "Yes, my dear brother, I have found the moon in my heart and the stars in my eyes, and I hope you will soon do the same."

After dinner, Dante and Zi spoke together outside while Zia and Fabia talked inside the tent. Dante told Zi, "I am very much in love with your sister and will ask her to be my wife."

Zi replied, "My sister, I love very much. Her wishes are mine. If my sister should ever be offended, all the

Gods in Heaven could not save you from my revenge. We are bonded like the earth and the sky and you could never separate us."

"I hear your words," said Dante. "I respect you for speaking your mind. You can rest assured I will never offend your sister but only love her as she well deserves."

Their talk brought forth a mutual respect between Dante and Zi. Dante found Zi to be as strong willed as he, with the potential to become a great warrior and leader among men. Dante told Zi about the bloody battles with neighboring tribes, and Zi listened intently to his every word. Dante explained he had lost more than two thousand men against the Adamites, a tribe who claimed to be from royal blood and laid claim to the vast region the two tribes occupied. The Adamites, he explained, claimed their peace was interrupted by a prince named Satan, and anyone who wasn't an Adamite was part of Satan's domain and had no right to the "holy land." Dante lowered his head when he spoke of the many close friends who had died beside him in battle. When he finished speaking, Zi was very impressed by Dante's compassion and courage and approved of his relationship with his sister.

Zia confided to Fabia that she was very fond of Dante. Fabia laughed, "With all due respect my naïve friend, my brother is like the many wild horses he captures. He has many women and not one woman has ever been able to tame him. He is stubborn as a mule, strong as a horse, and floats like a butterfly from one nest to another."

Zia responded, "He has now met the one who can tame him. His wings will be clipped forever, and only in my nest will he lay. There will not be many wives but only one. He has captured my heart, but now I own his soul. Perhaps it is my brother you should be concerned about, rather than me and Dante."

"Your brother is a virgin," laughed, Fabia. "I like him very much. Before the sun shall rise, he will know more about a woman than he ever expected."

"I have never had a female friend outside the family," said Zia. "I hope we can become friends. This whole experience is all new to me. I am not certain what one woman calls another woman that betrays her but I am sure there is a word for it. Both you and Dante are experienced in the ways of other people and we are not. But I have learned very fast since your brother first kissed me. I love my brother very much so you dare not disrespect him or you will have me to deal with. And I just might find the lost word I just spoke of. If he stays with you tonight make sure the sun shines on his heart in the morning."

Fabia never had a woman challenge her in such a way. She seemed appalled someone outside royalty would speak to her like that. She was the king's daughter and always had her way with everyone except for her brother. He was the only one who could put her in her place. But she dared not disrespect Zia for the sake of Dante's wrath. She forced a smile on Zia although she would have loved to slap her across the face. She assured Zia her brother was in good hands. Shortly after her conversation with Zia, Fabia took Zi to her own tent where they spent the night together.

* * * * *

Bubba and Lucy enjoyed their garden. They loved to plant a seed, nurture it, and watch it grow. There was something special about putting their hands into the earth and tilling the soil. The earth belonged to God, they agreed, and the vegetables that grew out of the dirt were part of God's gift to them. They never forgot to give thanks before each meal.

Lucy was aging very gracefully. She was still an attractive woman. Her hair was gray and the fine age lines on her face were dignified by grace and not by toil or worry. She had never lost her inner beauty that sparkled through her smile and eyes. Bubba's hair and beard were long, white, and unkempt. After a windy day in the yard, Bubba would often walk inside with his hair standing straight above his head and his clothes smelling like some of the many animals on their property.

Lucy made him wash in the spring before coming inside. As much as Bubba loved Lucy he still disliked being told what to do. What disgruntled him the most was that Lucy was always right. He had never forgotten what God had once told him when he had complained about her hair smelling like fresh fruit and berries. He took everything Lucy said to heart.

He had walked with a limp for so long he had forgotten he had one. He wore leather sandals and he never gave a thought to the fact his feet were different. And neither did his children. He had explained to his children that God give him special feet and no two people God created were just alike. In their adolescent years he loved to pull his sandals off and chase the children while walking and quaking like a duck.

Almost every day Bubba found something to give to Lucy to express his love. Lucy still had the pearls Bubba had once given her years ago, and Bubba proudly displayed the golden nugget above the fireplace. Many times it was very difficult for Bubba to find something different for Lucy. He had become a master craftsman and carpenter, and his house was full of leather and wood artifacts. Lucy constantly created gifts from pottery and cloth, and often surprised him with new recipes for the dinner table.

Bubba had practically picked every flower in the wild and when couldn't find different flowers, he always knew the seashore brought new life each morning. Their walls were covered with art from the beach. Once Bubba brought Lucy a dead twig from a tree. Lucy thanked Bubba for the twig and walked around the house, looking for a place to put it.

"It's very beautiful," said Lucy.

Bubba laughed, "It's just a lifeless twig. I was only joking."

Lucy responded, "The fact you were thinking about me is all that matters."

Giving was an important aspect of their lives together. They had taught their children that in order to receive one must first give. They encouraged the children to make gifts for one another and after they made something they really liked, it was important to give it away. The smile from a sibling was the reward for giving, they explained.

* * * * *

Bubba and Lucy were tending the garden when they saw the royal carriage crossing the river. Lucy had gathered a basket full of tomatoes when she stood and pointed toward the river.

"After three days our children have come home."

"I see only one in the carriage. Where is Zi? I send Zi to watch over his sister, and whom shall I send next to watch over him?"

"My dear husband," exclaimed Lucy, "we should be

glad Zia has returned after only three days. We have no power over our children. They are free spirits. They can do as they will. Have you not seen Mikia, Celeste, and Michael stand at the watchtower hour after hour and observe the Canites. It is only a matter of time until they also cross the river."

Bubba gave an angry groan.

Lucy snapped, "That is just like you, to only groan when you think of nothing else to say."

Bubba groaned again, this time louder.

Lucy gathered her vegetables, gave Bubba a disapproving look and angrily hurried out of the garden.

Bubba's and Lucy's relationship had its moments. They sometimes bickered but never quarreled at any length. If they disagreed on a particular matter they would sit down and discuss it together. If they could not come to terms, they prayed together, and it was quickly resolved.

Later that night Lucy imitated Bubba's groan while preparing dinner. Bubba groaned back with a smile and the two embraced one another.

* * * * *

Fabia asked Zi to spend another night, just the two of them. Zia had already left for home that morning after three days with Dante. The four had been together constantly, and Fabia requested another night with Zi in her arms. Zi didn't object. It wasn't like he had a lot to do on Kismira. He was totally bored with Kisrima and would stay forever if she wished. In fact, the thought of returning home made him ill. The choice between milking a goat or lying in bed with a beautiful woman was an easy decision for Zi to make.

Fabia had finally met a man who agreed with

everything she said, one who would do anything she asked, and she relished every moment of it.

Fabia's past was filled with many lovers, boyfriends, and suitors, but all her relationships were short lived. She was beautiful and rich, but was running out of Canite men who were possible suitors. Most knew she was spoiled and was hard to get along with her. If she couldn't have her way with men, she got rid of them, and if they catered to her, she had no respect for them. If a man jilted her, she would lie to her father about the real circumstance and her father would have them flogged for offending her.

Zi had come along at the right time for Fabia. The fact Zi did things out of kindness with no ulterior motives was one quality Fabia loved. She found him soft-spoken, unpretentious, assertive without being overbearing, and sexy without knowing it. He was like a refreshing breeze, totally different from the boring Canite men in the village. The fact Dante liked him made him even more attractive. Her brother had never approved of any of the men she had previously dated. Dante, who respected few men, detested cowards and men without conviction or courage.

* * * * *

Fabia began weaving a web to snare Zi. He was innocent and naïve, the perfect subject she could mold like a clay bowl into her own liking. But she realized she couldn't treat Zi like her past lovers or she would have to bear the wrath of Dante, and perhaps Zia.

Her first step was to ask Dante what Zi really thought about her, hoping he could share some insight to Zi's true feelings. She knew Zi and her brother talked a great deal in private, and perhaps Zi had said something about her.

Fabia often despised Dante but also respected him. He was the first to reprimand her, but he defended her if need be. She had for the most part respected his advice and opinion.

She found Dante at the stable and asked about Zi. Dante said, "My dear sister, you are like a basket of mixed nuts. And your past lovers are cakes that you have made from those nuts. You can eat the entire fruitcake, but before you are finished, you will find a slice that displeased you. Zi is a man of principal. He is a man who looks me directly into the eye when he talks. He is a man that you will never be able to control. And he is a man that is far too good for you."

Fabia was stunned. She stood speechless as anger swelled inside of her. "And you, my dear brother, I am sorry that I came to you. I will never ask your opinion again. You are nothing but a complete jackass."

Fabia turned and stormed out of the tent, more determined than ever to prove Dante wrong. She vowed Dante would see the day that Zi would be eating out of her hand.

* * * * *

Zi knew Fabia would never outwit him. He had never had a romantic relationship but had grown up with three sisters, which had taught him a great deal. He never argued for argument sake. He found it easier to let someone think he or she was smarter than to waste time trying to prove himself. He realized from the outset Fabia was pretty much an act, and he played along with her game. He let her think she was in control but knew he was on top and would eventually win in the end.

Zi remembered watching a spider get caught in its own web when he was growing up, and Fabia reminded him of the spider. He would let her get caught in her own web. Bubba had often told him, in private, a game must first be played with women because women did not think the same as men, and in order to win the game one had to think like a women.

Zi brought all his home training and expertise to the table. He genuinely liked Fabia. He was smitten by her beauty, charm, and her devilish ways. They were total opposites and he loved every minute of it.

The last night together was one he would think about for many nights. They spent a cozy night inside her tent, wrapped into one another's arms, listening to the sound of the ocean and watching the candles flicker, feeling her heart beat against his. She asked him questions about his family, which he thought was suspicious, but he didn't comment. She wanted to know if he had ever known Calio, and he instinctively answered *no*, remembering his father's request.

Zi thought it odd Calio left Kismira without saying goodbye to anyone and left in the middle of the night but never questioned his parents' explanation. Zi later informed Zia to deny she knew Calio and she agreed to do so. Both were suspicious about Calio's sudden departure but had never discussed it.

Zi didn't care about Fabia's motives for quizzing him. He could only think about his on desires. The intoxicating scent of her perfume and the taste of her painted lips was all that mattered.

* * * * *

The following morning, Dante took Zi to the stables where they talked and looked at horses. Zi didn't know the difference between a colt and a mare but listened while Dante talked about his love for horses. Zi quickly developed affection for them just by listening to Dante.

Dante showed Zi a sleek black stallion and offered it to Zi as a gift. Zi declined, stating he hadn't done anything to warrant such a gift and didn't believe in taking something not earned. Dante respected the comment.

"Well," Dante laughed, "you can put a hard days work in for your horse if it makes you feel better." He then asked Zi to help him round up a few horses that had wandered into the countryside.

Dante spent the remainder of the afternoon teaching Zi how to ride a horse and rounding up the strays before Zi returned home on his horse.

After Zi left that morning, Fabia left to see her father.

The king had anxiously awaited her visit. He dismissed her servants and the two talked in private.

"What have you to tell me, my little one?"

"He knows nothing about the disappearance of Calio."

"Are you sure?"

"Yes, he does not know how to lie. He has never been taught. He is as innocent as a butterfly and sweet as honey. And his family never heard of Calio. They are poor and uneducated as you guessed."

"And where is the rest of his family?"

"His father claims God is the only father he knows. And he and his wife descended from the Heavens like a leaf falls from a tree."

The king gave a hearty laugh. "They are a very strange couple. Perhaps they came from one of the many goats that roam freely on their property or the hawk that soars over the river."

The king took a more serious tone. "Or perhaps they

are spies from the homeland. I don't trust them. The fact they have no origin is like a nasty fly buzzing around my head."

"I feel very guilty, almost like a spy myself. I hope this matter is over."

The king laughed, leaning back in his chair, rolling his eyes for a moment, then bringing his eyes back on his daughter.

"And when has my little precious one ever felt guilty about anything? I certainly hope you have no intentions of seeing him again."

"I am very fond of him. He is more than meets the eye."

"I believe you and your brother have lost any sense the gods have blessed you with. My son I have not seen in three days. I hear he shows the other twin around the village like she is some princess."

"Yes, Dante is very serious about her and she just might very well be your first princess."

The king put both his hands on the armrest of the chair and struggled to lift himself, but instead settled back into his chair and pointed an angry finger at Fabia. "I will never stand for such a thing. Tell your brother I would like to talk with him right away."

The king lifted his arm, waving his hand in a gesture for her to leave. "Now go before you further upset me."

Fabia turned and walked away with saying another word, but smiled to herself as she left. She detested her father but loved him in a strange way she couldn't understand. Her mother had died when she was five and she had always suspected her father had a hand in her mother's death. She loved to antagonize her father because of what he had done to her mother, but soon the king would pay for all his past sins . . . without her help.

Within a few months, Bubba and Lucy found Dante at their doorstep asking for the hand of Zia. He had come on horseback, but with a mule in tow that carried many gifts for the family, as was custom in the Canite tribe. Zia knew he was coming that afternoon and observed from the watchtower with her brother and sisters as Dante spoke to Bubba and Lucy at the entrance of their home. She had not informed her parents of their impending marriage, and his arrival came as a surprise to Bubba and Lucy.

Dante knelt on one knee in front of Bubba and Lucy. "I come very humble, and bring many gifts to show my love for your daughter, and ask your acceptance and approval to be married."

"The gifts we cannot accept," said Bubba.

Dante stood and walked to the mule. "I have many fine gifts, gold and silver, and much more."

Before he could untie the straps to the gifts, Lucy walked to Dante, putting her hand gently on his.

"My husband is right. We understand it may be your custom, but our daughter's hand is not for sale."

Dante turned to Bubba and Lucy, falling on one knee, raising his eyes, and gesturing with an outstretched arm in the direction of Zia.

"What shall I say or do that will win your approval?

"I do not approve of the Canite way of life," said Bubba. "But I wish not to pass judgment. We are only concerned with the welfare of our daughter. She has now lived in your world but a short time, and knows little about other people."

Dante stood, raising both hands in a humble gesture. "What is it that you wish?"

"We wish that our daughter be happy," said Lucy.

Zia watched and waited patiently with her siblings while Dante talked to her parents. She wished she could hear what they were saying but could only hope her parents would give their blessings.

"They have refused the gifts," said Makia.

"They enjoy living in poverty," Michael said sarcastically.

"I would give anything to see inside those bags," commented Celeste.

"I would like to hold just one gold coin in my hand for the first time," said Michael.

Zia laughed and turned to Michael and her sisters. "I will own all the gifts very soon, I hope, even the mule. One day the village will be mine and all of you shall share my wealth. Dante is like raw dough I only have to bake in my own fashion."

"Look, Zia," said Celeste, very excited. "Dante is smiling and kissing our mother's hand."

Zia turned her eyes on Dante. He smiled and lifted his arms toward the sky in a gesture of joy. Zia jumped up and down, then turned and hugged her sisters before running down the steps toward Dante's waiting arms.

* * * * *

The king did not approve of the engagement but had no choice but to give his blessing. He knew Dante was stubborn, and nothing he could say would change his son's mind. There were many beautiful women in the Canite tribe, especially the daughters of the king's most trusted and wealthy friends. He had hoped his son would marry one of the Canite noble and was very distraught at the choice of a poor peasant woman to be princess.

The Canites made their living from farming, pottery, jewelry, furs, and a host of other trades, and each were taxed with a portion going to the king. He had become very wealthy and was suspicious of anyone outside his control, such as Zia. He suspected she was just after her son's money. Zia attempted to put his suspicions to rest over dinner one night when she said, "I only want to make your son happy and become a good Canite wife, and I will always serve the king with honor and obedience."

Zia had no intention of serving the king, much less being obedient to his will. She just told the king what he wanted to hear.

* * * * *

Zi had since joined the king's army as a lieutenant, but not without earning his rank. He was quick to master the sword and proved to be an excellent horseman. During practice maneuvers in the field, he outwitted his adversaries and proved to be an excellent military strategist. He suggested to Dante he should consider building a naval fleet to secure the neighboring waterways and Dante agreed.

Zi enlisted the help of Michael and Makia. Michael knew nothing about warfare but was good with details, and Makia was an excellent artist. The three drew up plans for a unique warship with iron guns and multiple sails. While Zi and Michael worked on the design of the ship, Makia sketched out the details and painted the final ship design on canvas. The three named the ship Caligastia to appease the king.

Dante presented the proposal to the king with Zi by his side, giving Zi credit for the design. The king liked the plan and gave his approval. Zi wore the Canite military uniform and, through his devotion to the military, won the respect of the king. It was no surprise to anyone when Zi asked for the hand of Fabia. They had been living together for a year. The king gave his blessing and demanded no dowry. Zi's loyalty to the military was enough dowry for the king, who put Zi in charge of building his first ship and promoted him to captain.

Zi's loyalty dismissed the king's suspicions about the family. He would never put a spy in charge of his naval fleet, but reserved the thought Zi's family was hiding something. He often awoke during his sleep and said to himself with a laugh, "Yes, their parents just fell to earth like a dropping from a bird."

The king decided both Dante and Fabia would be married in the same ceremony. Zi and Zia were very happy about his decision. As twins and brother and sister, they loved one another dearly. When they were children they vowed they would always remain loyal but never dreamed the day would come when they would be married together.

The Canites began celebrations a week before the wedding. The streets rang out with gaiety and laughter. The king participated in many of the activities and gave lavish dinner parties for his children. The Canites were soon to have a long-awaited princess, a very beautiful one who had won the admiration of the working class and a few nobles. She mingled with the merchants and talked to the poor while Dante stood by her side in awe that she was so well liked. Many of the Canites had known Fabia since she was a child and had little use for her. To the Canites she was nothing but a spoiled brat and had always thought herself above the common people. Fabia resented the attention her soon-to-be sister-in-law received and made a futile attempt to befriend the commoners. But it was too late; they quickly saw through her. She was, however, determined to make a successful attempt at marriage but the more she got to know Zi, the more she felt it was he who was manipulating her. She saw how his sister got anything she wanted out of her brother and how Zi seemed to always get what he wanted out of her in the end. She felt that any influence she may have had among the Canites was slowly slipping away since Zia arrived and had last-minute doubts about marrying Zi. The so-called poor little boy and girl from across the river were smarter than the credit she had given them.

Bubba and Lucy declined most invitations to participate in the wedding celebrations except for the one dinner party in their honor. However, Michael, Makia, and Celeste wasted little time in joining the festivities. They found friends their ages and stayed in the village with Zi and Zia until the eve of the wedding.

* * * * *

On the wedding day, Zi and Zia were alone in the bedroom of their parents' home. The family was busy preparing for the wedding and the twins wanted to spend a few moments together. They had both spent the night there as a last farewell to their parents and at the urging of Makia and Celeste. This would be the last time the family would be together as they were before. Her family would never again know her as Zia but as Princess Zia. It was an emotional time for the family, one of joy and tears.

Both Zi and Zia were worried about each other. Zia believed her brother loved Fabia, but thought the wedding was just a big game for Fabia to gain attention. Zi was not insulted by his sister's remarks. She was his best friend and confidant. There was only honesty and trust between the two.

Zi conceded Fabia was a little spoiled and he understood why she was concerned. He told Zia that Fabia would at least be faithful, a quality he didn't see in Dante. A woman could have only one husband but a husband could have many wives. He heard Dante loved women, and one wife would never be enough for him.

Zia told her brother, "Do not worry. I am well in control. Dante will never have another woman in his life."

Zi and Zia embraced. Zia wiped a small tear from her brother's eye and laughed, "I cannot ever remember my brother crying."

"Please do not tell anyone," said Zi with a chuckle. "It will certainly ruin my military career."

Zia kissed her brother on the cheek. "Your tears are like a refreshing raindrop from Heaven. And only God will ever know our secret."

"A man that cannot cry will never grow to be a man," said Lucy, standing in the doorway.

Zi and Zia turned and looked at their mother.

"You have ears like an elephant," said Zi.

"And eyes like Gork," laughed Zia.

"The proper name for such a thing with ears and eyes is often called mother," said Lucy with a pleasant smile.

Lucy entered the room with a string of pearls and motioned for Zia to turn around. Lucy put the pearls around Zia's neck. "These are the pearls your father gave me many years ago. He worked very hard diving into the sea for them. It is because of his hard work you and Zi were born," she said with a laugh.

"They are very beautiful, Mother. Are you sure you want me to have them? I know they mean a lot to you."

"Nothing means a lot to me except the welfare of my children," responded Lucy. "Your father quickly agreed that he wanted you to have them."

Zia turned, facing her mother. Lucy removed a brush from her pocket, turned Zia around and brushed her hair.

"I am very well pleased your face is not painted."

"Yes, Mother, my face looks like a dried fig without color."

"It is only temporary for the wedding, and it pleases your father. Tomorrow you can paint your face purple if you wish."

"Where is Father?" asked Zi. "The carriage will be here soon."

"Your father is in the barn milking the goats," said Lucy. "You both need to bid him goodbye. He is very upset his children are leaving him."

Zia put her arms around her mother. Lucy embraced her. She then raised her eyes to Zi before she had broken the embrace. "Put your arms around your mother," said Lucy to Zi. He quickly stepped forward and embraced his mother.

"I love you, Mother," said Zi.

"And I you, my son. I hope your life will be full of love and happiness."

"I have but one question, Mother," said Zi.

Lucy touched her son's face, looking into his eyes.

"You have not asked me a question in many years, and now speak, for I would like to answer your question."

"Both my sister and I have heard the word love many times now since the Canites have arrived, and I have told Fabia I love her and still I do not understand the meaning of this word love."

Lucy gave a sigh, turned her eyes upwards, and walked to the window. From the window she could see Bubba milking the goats just inside the barn. She hesitated for a moment and then turned toward her children.

"That is a very difficult question to answer," replied Lucy. "It took me a long time to love your father. A man thinks differently from a woman. True love does not come quickly. Love is like a flower that needs to be nourished and watered before it blossoms."

"When Dante touches me," replied Zia, "I get these small bumps on my arms, the size of pumpkin seeds."

"And I, Mother," added Zi. "I do nothing but dream about Fabia all day and night."

"You both have heard the thunder in your heart and have felt the lighting in your eyes, but that is not true love. It is only temporary. True love is only known when two hearts unite with the spirit of God. But my children have a long way to go before that happens. Often you may detest the person that you claim to love and many times this one will make you mad and angry. For now, my children only see the rising sun and not the storms ahead. And there will be many. Love only begins after the thunder and lighting has gone, and yet you still stand in the pouring rain, waiting patiently on the sunshine. I guess that is where love begins and where it goes from there is determined by the choices you make."

* * * * *

Bubba was still milking when he saw Zia standing in the barn. "You look very beautiful," said Bubba, only glancing in her direction for a moment.

"Thank you for the pearls," said Zia.

"Each day, Zia, you look more and more like your mother when she was your age, said Bubba without looking at Zia and continuing to milk the goat.

Zia walked to her father, kneeling beside him, lifting her wedding dress slightly above her knees to keep it off the dirt. She put her hand on her father's. "Stop milking the goats and look at me, Father."

Bubba lifted his eyes to Zia.

"I love you, Father."

"And I love you too, Zia. And this man, Dante, I know little about."

"And whose fault is that, Father? You have had many opportunities to get acquainted."

"And I was very foolish not to speak to him concerning my daughter," exclaimed Bubba.

Zia reached up and touched her father's cheek, turning his face toward hers. "You fail to realize I am not a child any more, but a woman in search of her own destiny and happiness."

Bubba took Zia's hand into his. "Do you remember the first time I took you into the sea? You were only about five years old. You jumped into the water without thinking. The water was deep and you had not learned to swim."

Zia lowered her eyes and looked up at her father. "Yes, I remember very well."

"I will never forget the helpless fright on your face. You fell underneath the water and when you surfaced you yelled the words, 'Father, help me.' I reached down and plucked you out of the water. You were naked and shaking, crying aloud. And you put your arms around me so tight I will never forget it."

"Oh, Father," said Zia. "I know what you are thinking, that I will never need you again. Only someone like you would remember an incident that happened so long ago, but I do remember. But make no mistake, Father, I will always need your love, and come to your arms when I am afraid."

Bubba put a tender hand on her face. "Once you become a parent, and only then will you understand what I am saying."

Bubba saw Zi standing just inside the barn. He and Zia stood as Zi walked to his father and sister. "The carriage is here," said Zi.

Zia turned toward her father and laughed. "Your first-born son is leaving but you seem not so concerned with him as you are with me."

"He is a man," responded, Bubba. "He can take care of himself. And yes, I am concerned about his welfare. Zi knows I love him more than I love myself, but to a man these words need not be spoken."

Zia laughed. "One day, Father, I may remind you of the words you have spoken . . . that a man is stronger than a woman and needs not the soft touch of his father and a shoulder to cry upon."

"You will make a great princess," replied Bubba. "And yes, I agree with you. I hope one day, Zi comes to rest on the shoulder of his father."

Bubba removed a gold nugget from his pocket and handed it to his son. Zi took the nugget in his hand and looked at his father.

"That small rock is worth more than all the gold in the world," said Bubba. It was your mother's first gift to me. And only a son would I give it to. May it always be a reminder that it's the small things in life that count the most."

"Thank you, Father," replied Zi.

"Go now," said Bubba. "I have goats to milk and cheese to make."

Bubba stood with a bucket of milk in his hand and watched his children run toward the waiting carriage that would take them across the river and change their lives forever.

* * * * *

The wedding took place on the seashore at sunset. The ceremony was simple but elegant because Zia wanted it that way. The king wanted the wedding to be held in his temporary quarters, but Zia objected, stating "Who is getting married, you or me?" Zia's arrogance only confirmed the king's opinion his soon-to-be daughter-in-law was a person with whom to be reckoned. He was rarely challenged and was angered by her comment in front of others until Zia did a half bow and said, "Only if it pleased the king." The king recognized Zia had made the statement only to save him embarrassment and later told Dante, "She is very wise and even more crafty. She would perhaps make a better general in the army than a good wife."

Zia planned her wedding with little regard to Canite custom. She had Makia do the floral arrangements that included flowers over a large archway overlooking the sea. Michael and Celeste helped build the elaborate set including a straw walkway which led to the altar where the king and families would be seated. She wanted an open ceremony so all the village people, rich or poor, could attend and feel part of the ritual.

Zia had torches distributed throughout the hillside, and at sunset the Canites lit the torches and waved them overhead while they softly sang *The Battle Hymn of Canites*. As the hymn echoed across the countryside, two horse-drawn carriages made their ways through the small winding village streets to the seaside altar. The procession was accompanied by a thousand of Dante's best Canite soldiers in official military dress, marching to the beat of a military band. Thousands gathered alongside the streets to cheer and to get a glimpse of their new princess.

Zia wore an elegant silk dress her sisters had made and the string of pearls given by her mother. A crown of colorful flowers adorned her hair, while carrying a single white rose in her hand. Fabia made certain she wasn't outdone by Zia. She was dressed in black and wore as much gold and silver as she could find places to put them. Dante and Zi wore blue military dress, each having a silver sword strapped to his waist.

The wedding was the climax of a full day of dancing, celebrations, and sacrifices to the gods. When the four joined hands, the king stood and spoke in his native Arabic language before a Canite priest delivered the wedding vows. In a few short moment, the week full of activities had quickly come to an end although there would be singing and dancing in the streets way into the night.

After the wedding, Bubba's family was escorted to the king's castle for a private dinner. The entourage of colorful carriages, decorated for the wedding, carried the newlyweds and the king's closest friends and family members. As the carriages made their way through the narrow streets they were greeted with congratulatory cheers from the villagers. Bubba and Lucy dreaded the dinner party. They had seen it all before and knew what to expect. It had been an emotional day for the two of them. All they wanted to do now was go home and relax. But they had no choice but to attend the dinner party and make the best of it to please everyone. They had already said their goodbyes to Zi and Zia and had little left to say.

Their ride home that night was mixed with ambivalence and a hint of melancholia. The children had stayed in the village for the night, and it would be the first time in years Bubba and Lucy came home to a house void of laughter and gaiety. They both realized the time would soon come when all their children would be gone, and Kismira would never be the same without them. That time came sooner than expected.

Over the next five years, Makia and Celeste found mates within the tribe, married and had children of their own while Michael elected to remain single. Michael and his friend Joshua made a small fortune brokering goods and wares to the local merchants. Zia and Dante completed their palace and found time in between to have six children. Fabia had miserably failed in her mischievous plans for Zi. Contrary to her expectations, it was Zi who always had the final word. They often fought and sometimes bickered for days at a time over trivial matters. Fabia had given birth to five children. Zi expected Fabia to stay at home and play the role of an obedient Canite wife. She loved her children but detested the fact she took a secondary role and was no longer in the limelight. She had gained weight after the third child and seldom dressed as before. She also saw no reason to wear makeup, which angered Zi.

Zi had built a splendid home equal to any of the residences owned by the Canite nobility. Since money was of no concern, Fabia left homemaking to her many servants and spent most days drinking wine with the few female friends she had left. She seldom saw Zia or talked with her in-laws. She detested Zi's family. Zi had hoped Fabia and Zia would become close friends through the years, but he gave up such expectations. He was working on his third ship for the king and was in charge of the king's emerging Navy. He worked long hours, and often spent the night at the port, which further added to their marital problems.

The children became involved in raising their own families and rarely visited their parents. Lucy, however, made occasional visits to the village where her family was always excited to see her. She was escorted by a royal carriage and treated with respect among the Canites. She enjoyed going to the marketplace and visiting her grandchildren with or without Bubba who detested going into the city.

The Canite population quickly multiplied over the next decade, and what was once a small village developed into a bustling city. The king created an import and export business where ships from all over the world sold their merchandise and goods. Egypt and Greece had become major empires, and the countries exchanged not only goods but ideas and technologies. The Canites welcomed new ships into their ports daily. Canna soon became a hub of commerce in the Mediterranean and a diverse melting pot of different cultures and races. Many who came to Canna made it their home.

Zia made sure her parents prospered from the busy seaport. She made Michael Chief Magistrate in charge of taxes, and her parents were given a percentage of the tariffs imposed on the ships.

The king had installed a Council of High Elders which made and enforced the laws and advised him on personal and business matters. Canna was divided into sections and the king appointed a governor for each province. Normally the governors were also High Elders. There were twelve High Elders and one Chief Elder who wore a black hooded robe, which distinguished him from the others who wore white.

The Elders ruled with great power and often made decisions in their own provinces without consulting the king. But the powers that be never stopped Zia from speaking her mind to the council when she thought an injustice had been done. She wielded great wealth and power and ruled with influence not normally afforded a woman. She was both loved and feared among the Canites.

Floggings and public executions were commonplace. Zia often appeared in the king's court in defense of someone she thought had been done an injustice and overrode the High Elders' decision. She was very outspoken, and the king tried to avoid confrontation with her. To him she was a big headache, but she was also the mother of his much-beloved grandchildren and he dared not offend her. He once told the Elders, "She has the presence of an angel but the wicked tongue of a serpent. Your day will go easier if you just agree with her."

The three sisters never forgot the humble roots from which they were born. Zia credited her mother and father for raising her with dignity and pride, which had prepared her for what she considered a public relations role. Zia put Makia in charge of art and design for the city projects. She was also made curator for the king's castle.

She made Celeste her personal assistant in charge of all her social functions until Celeste became pregnant with her eighth child and retired to a job as mother and housewife.

The sisters would often gather in Zia's private chamber, gossiping and giggling like children when no one was listening. They painted one another's faces and loved combing and styling the other sisters' hair.

Zia handed down many of the clothes and jewelry she had been given by Dante to her sisters. After all the years, it was still hard for the sisters to fathom their sister a princess. Although they had woven themselves tightly within the fabric of the royal family, they confided in no one outside their small circle and remained loyal to one another. When Makia reluctantly told Zia that Celeste had been abused by her husband, Zia had him publicly flogged. She always put family above title or prestige.

The property across the river remained undisturbed by time. Its beaches and seashore were still pristine and unspoiled. Zia forbade anyone to cross the river without her permission. The few curiosity seekers who were caught on the property were imprisoned or severely punished.

Bubba and Lucy were often invited to festivities in the city, but they always respectfully declined. Bubba occasionally accompanied Lucy to the marketplace but was quick to return home when their shopping was done. Prosperity and growth also had brought crime and violence to the city. Although Bubba and Lucy were considered part of the royal family, they wanted no part of the social life they saw in the city. They enjoyed walks on the seashore, simple meals, and working in their garden together. They purchased seeds from the market and had a beautiful garden full of tomatoes, corn, beans, and more. They enjoyed feeding and caring for the many sheep, goats, chickens and other farm animals, and knew each one by name. They missed Cocoa, who had died of old age, and often thought about Tonka.

There were no fences or boundaries for the animals that grazed and wandered anywhere they desired. The horses, pigs, goats, and other animals could easily be seen lazily basking in the sun on the beach or lying in the shallow waters of the river by the fishermen and merchants across the river. The Canites often laughed and commented about the stark contrast between the two properties only narrowly split by the river.

Bubba and Lucy were both resolved to a quiet and reclusive existence. The sounds of children laughing and playing that once filled the home had been replaced by the howling wind from the sea that drifted easily through the many cracks and into the house. The steps leading to the watchtower had decayed from age, and Bubba had closed it off. The front walls of the house had taken their toll from the wind off the seas and had crumbled away. The large wooden gates that stood on the outer wall of the house were rotten and now stood open to the sea. With each strong gust of wind another section of the roof was blown away.

Bubba and Lucy had no desire to repair their home. The children rarely visited, and to rebuild would erase all the good memories for which the house stood. He and Lucy had a kitchen and two small comfortable rooms in which they lived, and that was enough for them.

The reclusive Bubba, father of the princess, the eccentric old man who had strange feet and talked to his animals and claimed he had simply descended from the Heavens, fallen out of the sky and appeared on earth one day, was a constant mystery and source of gossip to the Canites. It was rumored among the citizens of Canna that Bubba had more gold than the king himself and lived like a squatter to hide all his wealth. It was common knowledge among the Canites Bubba received a portion of the tariffs, and rumor had it there was a secret vault full of gold below the run-down home.

Bubba, however, could have become a wealthy man over the years, but he instructed Michael, as Chief Magistrate, to secretly distribute most of his earnings to the poor, only retaining enough money for basic needs. Even Zia was never told of the arrangement.

One day King Caligastia summoned Zia to attend a meeting with the High Elders. He explained to Zia the seashore could no longer expand from east to west without the property of her father. There was no more deep water for the ships to moor, and the mountains blocked additional expansion to the west. He asked Zia to talk with her father and ask him to sell a portion of his property to the king.

The High Elders presented Zia with documents for their parents to sign and hinted her parents had little choice but to comply with the king's wishes.

"I will talk to my parents," said Zia. "But never think you can intimidate them into selling. I will ask for just enough property to meet your need and no more."

When Bubba saw Zia's carriage crossing the river he was very excited she was coming to pay a visit. She visited only a very few times since she had been married, and he quickly summoned Lucy when he saw Zia approaching.

After Zia explained the purpose of her visit, Bubba was very disturbed, but he showed little emotion. He explained to Zia that no amount of money could purchase the property. She respectfully argued it would be a personal favor to her and the king, and would greatly help the merchants avoid higher taxes.

Bubba told Zia, "This is the room where you took your first steps as a child. The seashore is where you gathered shells with your brothers and sisters and where you left your footprints. And the sea still whispers the name of our beloved Anna and carries her wreath."

Lucy intervened, saying, "Zia, we are very fortunate to have a daughter like you and we are both very pleased great wealth and power has not corrupted the daughter we raised from a baby, but hear your father's words. This is the earth you and your brothers and sisters took your first steps on, and we cherish the memory. We will not sell any part of Kismira to be corrupted by money and greed, and turned into another like that across the river. While the king's treasures lay in the earth, our treasures lie in our hearts and belong to God."

When Zia heard this she knelt beside her mother and wept like a child.

"I am sorry that I came with such a request," said Zia. "It was very foolish of me. It is because of you and Father I am who I am today. Will you forgive me?"

"We both love you, Zia, more than you will ever know," said Bubba. "You never need to ask forgiveness. You have done nothing but convey the king's wishes because of your desire to please."

* * * * *

Zia returned to the king that afternoon with the unfavorable news. The king was very angry after Zia had stated her parents' position.

"What are these treasures of the heart they so boldly proclaim? I have made them very wealthy and now they show me disrespect and no appreciation."

"I am very sorry," Zia explained to the king. "I did my very best and now let this notion be ended. My father can never be forced to sell."

After Zia left, the king called a secret meeting of the High Elders. It was decided no more royalties be paid to Bubba and his gold be secretly confiscated.

"When he has no more gold to hide within his vaults," laughed the king, "then he will be begging us to buy his land"

They agreed no one outside the council would know of the plans. They decided to select three thieves from the prison to carry out the mission and give them amnesty for the return of the gold and for their silence

A sentry was posted at the river crossing. After weeks of waiting the king received word Bubba and Lucy were crossing the river en route to the market. He then put his plan into action.

The thieves crossed the river and searched the home. They were instructed to load the gold onto a wagon and travel east where a boat would meet them and unload the treasure. But after a search of the home, no treasure was found. The thieves were surprised to find they themselves lived better than the princess's own father. They were ready to give up the search when one of the thieves found a false door leading to a cellar, a door Michael had installed years ago before the Canites had arrived. Certain they had found the secret vault, they pried open the door and entered. The cellar was dark, mildewed, and smelled of age. Spider webs and dust covered the many spears and handmade weapons hanging on the walls and ceiling.

After a quick search the thieves found a chest bound in leather straps in the corner of the room. Certain they had now found the treasure, they eagerly cut the straps and opened the chest. Inside the thieves found a silver sword with a gold handle. They dusted the sword and looked at one another in disbelief. The letter C was inscribed on the handle and it carried the royal Canite symbol.

The thieves immediately carried the sword to the king, who looked at the sword and wailed in anger. "The sword is that of my beloved Calio," he shouted. He then drew his own sword and stepped toward the thieves, pointing the sword at them. "Bring me the head of the one who lived across the river. I command you!"

The thieves pleaded with the king, explaining they were only petty thieves and not executioners, and they could never carry out such an order. The king soon regained his composure and agreed with the thieves. He had them returned to the dungeons to maintain their silence until he decided what his next move would be.

The king called a midnight meeting with the High Elders. Most of the Elders had known Calio since his birth, and were very angry his disappearance was kept a secret by Bubba and his family. It had been a mystery for many years. The king assumed his son and his escorts had been killed by bandits on the way to find the great river. Now the mystery was solved except for the circumstances of his death.

The High Elders were debating a course of action as the sun rose over Canna. They assumed Bubba had murdered Calio and he should be punished by death, but they couldn't decide how it would be carried out. Bubba's son, Zi, was captain over the king's navy not to mention his daughter was the princess, married to his son. The king doubted his own son, Dante, would carry out such an order.

The fact no treasure was found in Bubba's home raised the suspicion among the High Elders that the gold had gone elsewhere, perhaps into the pockets of Bubba's son, the Chief Magistrate, or to Zi or Zia. And the fact the family had covered up a murder now raised the circumstance that anything could be possible.

After two days of deliberation it was decided the most trustworthy in the king's command were his own personal guards. They were the gate keepers of his castle and under his direct authority. The king sent the guards before daybreak to arrest Bubba and bring him to the king's court for questioning. They decided they would take a course of action after talking with Bubba.

While the king and the High Elders waited that night, they discussed the consequences of an execution. The king feared his sons and daughters would turn against him, but the High Elders reminded the king that soon everyone would know about the murder of his son, and he would lose respect of the nobility if nothing were done about it. The Elders also reminded him he was king and he, not public opinion, should assert authority over the matter.

Bubba was brought into the court while the High Elders were still debating his fate. He had come freely, without restraints, and stood in front of the king with the High Elders seated on a long circular table adjacent to the king's throne. Many had never seen the reclusive man from across the river and were appalled by his appearance. His clothes were torn and his hands dirty from working in the garden. They observed his hands and feet and whispered among themselves as he stood before the king.

"I regret you would not sell part of your property as I requested," said the king. "You are a very wealthy man with many treasures."

Bubba replied, "The only treasure I have is within my heart."

The High Elders all grumbled among themselves at this answer, satisfied he was lying and would never reveal where his wealth was hidden.

The king then asked, "Did you murder my son, Calio?"

Bubba answered with a simple, "Yes."

"What have you to speak of this murder?" asked the king.

"Your son came as a friend to the family and deceived us. He attempted to abduct my wife, Lucy. He held her captive. When he drew a dagger from his belt, I killed him with a sword. There is no more to the story."

"You are a liar," shouted the king. "My son would do no such thing."

"He would say anything to save his own self," yelled one of the Elders.

"Yes," agreed another Elder, standing and pointing his finger at Bubba. "Calio comes from royal blood. In his veins flows the blood of many gods. He was blessed by the gods when he was born and now you have robbed him of his lawful inheritance to one day rule the kingdom."

"You and the so-called Elders," said Bubba, "are nothing but foolish old men who brood in your own misery because you do not know the real God, the one and only God, who lives within the hearts of men. No man is royalty except within his own mind. You are too busy hiding behind the painted faces of your women to discover the real truth about your existence."

There was a loud outcry among the High Elders. The Head Elder stood, and shouted, "Now blaspheme will be added to your treacherous deeds."

Another stood. "You have not only murdered the king's son but now insult the king in his very presence. Surely you will pay."

Bubba raised his eyes at the king. "And what do you say to one who speaks only the truth and whose grandchildren carry your blood and mine?

The king bowed his head and gave a heavy sigh. Raising his head and looking at the Elders, he said, "It is true I and this man are bonded by a fate I unfortunately cannot reverse. He shall be locked away until we have made a decision."

Before morning Zi and Zia heard of their father's arrest and went immediately to the king's court, demanding his release. The king had extra guards posted at the gates. Zia ordered they step aside and let her enter. When they refused, the Chief of the High Elders stepped from behind a wall, and stood between the guards. He told Zia the king was sick and he would not address the issue to anyone including her.

Zia walked a few steps and stood inches from the High Elder, looking directly into his eyes,

"It is you, Batholomew, who is behind this. If my father is not released I shall have your head on a silver platter."

"If that is your wish," he replied with a smirk.

Zia turned and stormed away, attempting to control her anger.

* * * * *

Zia awoke a servant, Eli, to hitch the horses to the

royal carriage, while Zi gathered his brother and two sisters and informed them of their father's arrest. After the children boarded the carriage, Zia instructed Eli to cross the river and take them to their mother's.

When the guards took Bubba into custody earlier that night they said nothing to Lucy or Bubba about finding Calio's sword or the circumstances of his arrest. Lucy paced the floor all night awaiting his return. When she heard the coach pull up and saw her children stepping down she knew something dreadful had happened. The children had never come together and in the middle of the night. Lucy waited at the door of her home. She saw the expression of their faces and her lips began to quiver.

"Father is alive," said Zia quickly to dispel any notions the worst had happened.

Zi and Michael took their mother by the arm and helped her back inside the house. After the children led their mother to a chair, Zia explained the nature of the arrest.

Lucy gasped and covered her mouth with her hand as soon as she heard the name Calio. Her eyes swelled full of tears when Zia told her about the sword found in the cellar.

"The king has accused our father of murder," said Zia. "I was very young but remember Calio very well. You told us he returned to his tribe. What is the truth?"

Lucy bowed her head for a moment and raised her eyes toward her children who stood silently and waited on an explanation. She had always been honest with her children and the fact she had lied to them had always tormented her. It was the only time she had ever lied to her children, and she prayed they would understand.

"It is true," said Lucy, trying to steady her hands.

The sisters knelt beside their mother to comfort her.

"What is true, Mother?" asked Zia, putting a reassuring hand on her mother's arm.

"It is true your father killed Calio and buried him in the woods."

The children gasped, speechless.

"But your father is not a murderer," she continued. "Calio kicked and beat me. He was trying to abduct me when your father killed him."

Lucy's eyes slowly passed on each of her children. "I have always been honest with my children. I hope you can forgive me."

After Lucy had explained Calio's death the children were relieved. To them it was a clearly a case of self defense. They felt certain the charges would be dropped after the king heard the truth. The children begged their mother to return with them until the matter was resolved, and she agreed. It was decided she would stay with Celeste, who had a modest home with six young children. There she would be less conspicuous than at Zi's or Zia's palace.

The following morning Zi and Zia returned to the king's court but were refused admittance. They were told by the High Elder the king was very ill. The twins left the king's court and traveled a short distance to the prison, which was heavily fortified. The guards came to attention when the royal carriage pulled into the entrance.

Zi and Zia entered through the gates without a problem but were stopped by the head guard. He was well past his youth, and his years as a warrior showed on his face. He gave a slight bow as Zia and Zi approached.

"My greeting to the princess."

"We have come for the release of my father," demanded Zia.

"I am sorry, but I have my orders from the king," replied the guard politely.

"Tell him to release our father. You have the authority," said Zia.

"Although he wears the uniform, he is not part of the Canite Army," said Zi. "He is a royal guard, not a military guard. His orders come directly from the king and only the king."

The guard graciously nodded his head and smiled at Zi for understanding and simplifying the matter.

"Well, you can tell the guard this, my brother," she said with a stern face and looking directly at the guard. "The so-called royal guards are but a few and the Canite Army many thousands. I certainly hope he quickly learns how to count."

The guard dropped his smile. Zia turned and stormed away. Zi nodded goodbye to the guard and followed Zia to the coach.

* * * * *

Dante refused to use military force against the guards. This greatly angered Zia. Her father had been imprisoned for almost a week now, and still the king refused to meet with his own son to discuss the matter. He had secluded himself inside the courts of his castle where he claimed to be ill, speaking only through one of the High Elders.

Dante sought a diplomatic solution. He suggested an open court or forum with the High Elders to openly discuss the matter. He sent a proposal to the king but after three days he had not received a reply. The children met nightly at Celeste's to discuss the crisis, leaving their spouses and children at home. They would stay all night and until daybreak, talking, hoping, and praying with their mother something could be worked out with the king.

Bubba's arrest created chaos among the Canites. There were those loyal to the king and those loyal to the princess. The king's supporters were the noble, older Canites, and those who remembered Calio. Most were wealthy merchants who controlled the commerce and trade upon which the king heavily relied for tax revenues. Those who supported Zia were the common people, the poor, and the younger Canites, who comprised most of the king's army.

Soon the bickering and arguing among the Canites turned into bloodshed when a royal guard was killed by one of the Princess Zia's supporters. In retaliation, a military guard was stoned to death by a group who supported the king. Blood soon spilled upon the streets. Riots, looting and fires broke out in the city. Dante ordered Zi to take a company of his best soldiers to restore order. Zi followed his orders and advised his men to be non-partisan and to use discrimination in dealing with the rioters. He reminded his men they were Canite civilians; he didn't want to escalate the situation.

Zia insisted her mother, her grandchildren, and all of her siblings move into the palace until order could be restored. Their husbands remained behind to protect their property.

The High Elders called a meeting with the king. They challenged his leadership, citing that doing nothing would lose support of the nobility. They reminded the King that without support of the nobility and the wealthy, his empire would be subject to collapse. They insisted the king have Bubba put to death immediately for the murder of Calio to restore order. An open court, they insisted, would only incite more riots.

After listening to the arguments, the king reluctantly issued an execution order. He ordered the beheading to be carried out early the following morning in fear that a delay would cause more strife and turmoil. He insisted the order be kept secret until it was over. After the meeting, the High Elders returned to their homes where one mistakenly told his wife about the execution. She in turn told her niece who supported the princess.

Within hours word was delivered to the princess's palace. Dante and Zi were patrolling the streets and had been gone for two days. It was far too dangerous for the princess or her family to ride into the city to search for them so the sisters asked Michael to go. He was not a warrior or soldier. In fact, he had never been on a horse. Michael, however, agreed to ride on horseback to find Dante or Zi. After he left, the family could do nothing but wait and pray. Lucy sat quietly, assuring her daughters Bubba would not be put to death. She had another plan but kept that secret to herself.

A few hours before daybreak, Michael hadn't returned. Lucy realized time was running out. She had thought about it all night and now she rose from her chair and looked at her sleeping children and grandchildren. She gently stroked one of her grandchildren's head and quietly slipped out of the house. She would have liked to have told her children goodbye but it would have been much too painful and she knew her children would object to what she was going to do.

She prayed for her children as she made her way up the steep incline toward the king's castle. She hoped one day they would understand and silently begged their forgiveness. When she reached the gates to the castle, she asked the guard permission to speak to the king. The guard at first refused.

"Tell the king Cali sent me and he will surely see me."

The guard recognized Lucy as mother to the princess and sent a messenger to the king. Lucy waited at the gate. In a few moments she was escorted to the king's chamber.

The king entered the court in his night robe, wiping the sleep from his eyes. Lucy was waiting in the chamber. The king sat, gave a heavy sigh and lifted his eyes on Lucy.

"Where did you hear this name, Cali?"

"Your wife, Sarah, called him Cali when he was born, but you changed his name to Calio."

"And my son told you this?

"Yes, he missed his mother greatly and told me of her untimely death."

"What did he say of her death?" asked the king.

"You and I both know the sad truth concerning your wife's death. She was poisoned by your own hand. Your son, Calio, never got over the death of his mother."

"My son would have never told you these things," snapped the king.

"How else would I know the name Sarah? He told me about your wife and much more I wish not to discuss," replied Lucy. "And there are other things about Calio I could say that would free my husband, but I chose not to speak of them."

"I would like to hear them if they concern Calio."

"To say them now would only dishonor my husband and my family," replied Lucy.

"Then what is the purpose of your visit if you choose not to say the words that would save your husband's life?

"I come to offer myself in exchange for my husband's life."

"That is preposterous," laughed the king.

"Hear me out," replied Lucy. "I was partly to blame for your son's death, although I did not use the sword that killed him. Your kingdom is divided. I wish not for my family to be destroyed by it. My death would restore peace and at the same time you would save face with the Elders and those loyal to you."

"You are a very brave woman," replied the king.

"My husband is a most holy man and his work is not finished in the kingdom of the living God. I fear not for my life, but for his. My life has been very rewarding and I am prepared to stand in his place now before my husband and others know I am here. I would rather them not plead for mercy."

The king gave a long thought to Lucy's proposal.

"I will agree under a few conditions," he said, gesturing with his finger. Will you sign a confession that you were responsible for my son's death so all will be satisfied?"

"I will sign whatever it takes to save my husband's life and to restore peace," said Lucy.

"Tell me these things about Calio that you refuse to speak of."

"I wish not to disrespect my family."

"You have my word I will never speak of them again."

Lucy took a step forward, cupped her hand together and lowered her head. She took a deep breath, paused for a second, raising her head and lifted her eyes on the king.

"You have a granddaughter. Her name was Anna," she said softly.

"How so?" asked the king. "And where is this so-called granddaughter?

"She drowned at sea many years ago," said Lucy as

her lips quivered at the mention of Anna. "She was only five years old." Lucy lowered her eyes. "She was so beautiful."

The king nervously shifted in his seat and leaned forward in his chair with one hand on his knee as though he was about to stand. "And just whom might Anna's parents be?" he asked with a hint of sarcasm.

"Your son, Calio abducted me, and took my womanhood freely without my consent, but first he beat me when I refused. Calio is the father."

"And what does your husband have to say about this?"

"He only knows that I was abducted and beaten. My husband came to my aid and killed Calio only in self-defense."

The king leaned back in his chair and scratched his chin while contemplating what he had just heard. In a few moments he spoke. "That is a very elaborate story. You slander my son's good name in order to save your own self, and perhaps your husband's as well. And I played right into your hands. Now, I guess a pardon is in order?"

"I speak only the truth. It was you that requested I speak, not I. And I still remain ready to go in my husband's place. My last words would never be a lie."

The king gave a heavy sigh. He snapped his finger and a lone servant standing nearby walked to the king and filled his cup with wine. He took a drink and then sat the cup down on the arm of his chair, and looked at Lucy.

"This decision is not without heavy burden," he said.

"I understand," replied Lucy.

"If you are not lying then perhaps one question may clear you of this matter and I will know that you speak the truth."

"And what question is that," asked Lucy?

"Since the day the Canites arrived, I have heard rumors you and your husband claim to have no ancestors and you claim to have been born from the gods. What is the truth of your origin?"

"It is no rumor, but the truth. My husband came first and then the one and only God created me to be with my husband."

The king grew very angry. He struggled to his feet under his heavy weight, and pointed a trembling finger at Lucy.

"You blaspheme the gods and expect me to believe such nonsense. I shall take this matter to the High Elders and see what they have to say."

The king then stormed out of the room, and Lucy was escorted to the king's garden to await her destiny.

Zi and a dozen of his elite soldiers had been patrolling the northern sector of Canna for two days and nights without sleep. It was the province of Mosul in which most of the looting and fighting took place. Dante was in the city, setting up a command center when Zi and his men caught a young looter with stolen goods in his hand. Dante and his men sat on their horses as the young looter stood before them, raising a sword. A crowd gathered, watching and waiting the outcome. Zi and his men had arrested over a dozen men that night, and Zi was growing tired and discontent. He pleaded with the looter to put down his sword and go home.

"You have arrested my brother for doing the same and who are you that I should trust?"

"I am Zi, captain in the king's navy, but tonight assist in restoring peace to Canna."

"I have heard of you. You are brother to the princess who rules without true Canite blood in her veins. I am poor and have stolen nothing but food to feed my mother."

"What gives you the right to take from another who may be also trying to feed his own family?"

"My father worked as a house servant to Tiberius, governor of Mosul and High Elder in the king's court. He told my father we should take what we need and be hungry no more, that all our taxes go to fatten the princess's pocket."

"Tiberius said this to your father?"

"Yes, he also said Canna is no longer ruled by the king or his son, but by the princess, who owns all the gold in Canna."

"Where is your father that I may speak to him?"

The young boy slightly lowered his head. "He was killed last night in a skirmish with soldiers.,"

"How old are you," asked Dante?

"Thirteen, sir."

"Take your food and go home but steal no more."

The boy hesitated, unsure of what he had just heard.

"Go, now," said Zi, "before I change my mind."

The soldiers watched the young boy gather the stolen goods and run away. Zi then turned his horse to face his lieutenant.

"You're getting soft," replied the lieutenant.

"No, Lieutenant," responded, Zi, "I'm beginning to see the picture."

"How is that, sir?"

"It seems Tiberius and perhaps others in the king's court have their own agenda. As much as I love my father, I find it hard to believe the Canites feel the cause is worth dying over. The High Elders were looking for a reason to divide Canna and my father is the perfect excuse. And with him dead they think they could more easily purchase Kismira to fatten their own pockets."

"Well spoken, sir."

Their conversation was interrupted by the sound of a galloping horse. Zi and his men watched as an obviously inexperienced horseman appeared out of the dark, into the moonlight, made an awkward wide arch and turned toward them.

"Isn't that your brother, sir?"

In a few moments Michael approached the soldiers, pulling hard on the reins of the horse in an attempt to stop. He could hardly catch his breath when he managed to stop the horse next to Zi.

"When did you learn to ride a horse, Michael?"

"Tonight, Zi. And after a full day and night I have found you."

"The news of our father is very bad. He is to be executed at daybreak, and we have only a few hours to secure his release."

Zi turned toward his lieutenant. "Find Dante and tell him to meet me at the king's castle, then you and your men go home and get some rest."

Overhearing the conversation, one of the soldiers spoke. "I shall be honored to ride with you, sir, in your time of need."

The other soldiers all quickly nodded their heads in agreement to go with Zi.

"Thank you," replied Zi to his men as they turned their horses south and headed for the king's castle.

* * * * *

Lucy sat in the courtyard just outside the king's main chamber awaiting an answer from the king. The courtyard was enclosed by a circular stone wall, and at the center stood a water fountain surrounded by flowers. The top of the atrium was open to the sky and Lucy sat peacefully with her hands on her lap, watching the moon and stars slowly slip away and give birth to the daybreak.

She had been waiting for almost an hour when two guards and a swordsman entered the courtyard. The tall, young swordsman saw it was Lucy who was to be executed and turned to one of the guards. "This is the mother of the princess, surely not a thief or murderer. I cannot carry out this order."

"It is by her own request she is to be executed," came a voice from the shadows of the courtyard.

The Chief High Elder was dressed in his traditional black robe and wore his hood over his head, partially covering his face. At first the guards did not recognize the High Elder.

"Who speaks there," ask one of the guards?

"Batholomew, Chief of the High Elders," came the reply as the High Elder stepped into the light where his face could be seen.

"Our apologies, sir. "

"The sentence much be carried out immediately."

The swordsman drew his sword and dropped it to the stone floor of the courtyard.

"Then find someone else to carry out the order, sir"

"I could have you also sentenced to death for disobeying an order from the king."

"So let it be," replied the swordsman.

Lucy lifted her eyes at the swordsman. "What is your name?"

"My name is Alexander," he said.

"Come, Alexander," said Lucy with an outstretched hand.

The swordsman walked a few steps to Lucy and took her hand in his.

"Do not be afraid," said Lucy. "I can see you are a man of great courage and conviction, and it is you I wish to carry out the order."

The swordsman dropped to one knee, put his other

hand on Lucy's, and bowed his head. "Then I will ask your forgiveness."

"I hold no animosity toward you, Alexander. You need not ask for forgiveness because you are already forgiven. May your life be full of peace and happiness."

Lucy stood and walked to the edge of the garden where she picked a flower and smelled it. She looked into the early-morning sky for a brief moment before turning toward Alexander and kneeling before him with the flower cupped in her hands.

A silence filled the air as Alexander lifted his sword from his side. Lucy smiled and lifted her eyes toward the last remaining star in the Heavens, then bowed her head. Alexander looked at Batholomew, who gave a nod to proceed. Alexander raised his sword but was interrupted when a yellow morning dove flew into the courtyard and perched on the tree limb just above him. The swordsman was momentarily taken aback by the sight of the unusual bird.

Lucy opened her eyes, looked at the dove and smiled. Alexander loosened his grip on the sword, lowered it and turned toward the High Elder walking toward him.

"Do it!" commanded the High Elder. "Or I will have your head. In one swift downward swing of the sword she was beheaded.

Alexander walked to the High Elder, dropping the bloody sword once again at his feet. "Her blood is on your hands, not mine, and I will never be in the service of the king again." He abruptly left the courtyard.

Lucy's body was quickly taken to a secret location where it was cremated. Her ashes were then tossed into the sea. The king thought this better than for her to become a martyr and her body perhaps paraded for days in the streets.

* * * * *

When Zi, Michael and his soldiers arrived, they were greeted by the Chief High Elder who stood on the steps of the castle with a dozen guards.

"I demand the immediate release of my father, and tell the king that I shall reduce his castle to smoldering ruins should he not release him."

"And who are you to think you have such power to do these things?"

"My men will follow my command, Batholomew, and I know now of your treacherous deeds by way of Tiberius."

"Neither you or princess are from royal Canite blood and you think you can rule over Canna at will and make a mockery of the king."

"I have no desire to rule Canna. I come only for the release of my father."

"Your father is a free man as we speak."

"How so?" asked Zi.

Before the High Elder could speak, Zia and her sisters approached by carriage, followed by Dante and a company of his soldiers. The sisters stepped out of the carriage and quickly stood beside to Zi and Michael.

The High Elder looked with disdain at the company of men Dante had brought with him. "Even the king's own son challenges his father."

Zi turned his eyes on his sisters. "He speaks our father is free."

"But our mother is missing," replied Zia. She then shifted her eyes to the High Elder. "Do you know the whereabouts of our mother, Batholomew?"

"She is gone," he said.

"What do you mean, gone?" asked Zi.

"She sleeps with the gods by her own will. She chose to die in place of your father."

Zia and her sisters gasped, and held one another to steady themselves. Zi drew his sword and raised it at the High Elder. "Surely you lie. I will cut your tongue out! Where is the body?"

"The king had her cremated," said the High Elder. Zi slowly lowered his sword, realizing the High Elder was telling the truth. He looked at Michael, who was speechless, and then turned his eyes at his sisters. Celeste had collapsed to her knees and both Zia and Makia were sobbing aloud.

"This can't be," Michael said to Zi as he tried to maintain his composure.

Zi was too shaken to respond. He could only put a comforting hand on his brother's shoulder.

The word of Lucy's death quietly filtered through the ranks of Dante's soldiers, and over them fell a calm, chilling silence; only the sound of sobs and grief filled the air.

* * * * *

Later the next day, Zia gathered the strength to address the issue and decided they would have nothing more to do with the king. She forbade their children to ever speak to him again. Zia told the king as she stood before him one last time, "When you are old and feeble, let the Council of High Elders be your comfort. And when your grandchildren never speak your name again, you can use all your wealth to buy gifts for the nobility."

The death of Lucy and the estrangement from his family haunted the king for many years. He eventually ended his life by drinking wine laced with poison.

* * * * *

Bubba made sure his farm animals were safe and away from the house. He called out for Gork, and within seconds Gork landed on his shoulder. He walked inside his home. His hands were trembling so badly it was difficult to hold the candle he had lit. He took a nervous breath, stood in the center of the kitchen and looked around as though searching for a place to put the candle. He slowly made his way to the bedroom where he and Lucy had shared their most intimate moments. He placed the candle on a table, and removed a bundle of blankets from a chest and piled them together in the center of the room. He retrieved the candle, tossed it into the pile of blankets and sat sat in his favorite chair in the corner of the room. His void and lifeless eyes watched the blankets ignite and burn. When his eyes began to water, he leaned over, brought his hands to his face and wept.

Regaining his composure, he raised his eyes toward the fire and watched the flames spread to the walls and slowly engulf the ceiling and spread into the other rooms. He raised himself up from his chair and walked quietly to the entrance, stopping briefly in the main room and looking at a painting of him and Lucy. He remembered Makia had painted it when she was twelve years old. He stood, looking at the painting while smoke drifted under the wall in front of him and traveled upwards over the picture.

The sound of hot crackling lumber rang throughout the house. He took one last look at the painting that now curled from the heat and burst into flames. His hair was singed and his face slightly blistered from the heat as he walked outside to a safe distance from the house. He sat on a stump he once used for chopping wood. Within a few minutes the house was engulfed in fire. A gentle wind from the beach fed the flames, lifting the black smoke high above the tree tops and sending it over the river.

Bubba quietly watched a lifetime of hard work and memories disappear before his eyes in a few minutes. Nothing inside now had value or significance.

He gazed at the watchtower as it collapsed and was numb from any emotion or feelings other than the grief that consumed his every thought. Life, he thought, was now useless, worthless, and void without Lucy to share it, and all purpose for living was gone as quickly as the watchtower. He felt no anger or resentment toward the king. He knew revenge would only destroy him. Lucy was gone forever like Anna and Tonka and no prayer could ever bring her back.

When he stood to leave he had no idea how long he had been sitting on the stump. He left the prison the moment he received word of Lucy's death without first searching for his children, and realized they were probably searching for him. Many Canites had already gathered on the riverbanks along Canna and were watching the huge fire, and he knew his children would be there any moment. He was too distraught to talk to anyone, even his sons and daughters. His only desire was to be alone until he could compose himself.

* * * * *

The summer evening was slowly turning into twilight as Bubba made his way along the winding edge of the foliage that curved along the beach and disappeared into the woods. With Gork on his shoulder, the two traveled until it was too dark to find the way. Gray clouds drifted above the treetops. A sprinkle of rain began to fall. Exhausted, Bubba lay down on the forest floor and curled up under a tree, resting his head on a clump of grass. The pain and loneliness he felt in the dark forest now swelled inside again. He felt like he had come full cycle . . . walked in a circle and ended up right where he had begun. He opened his eyes in the direction of the Heavens, but only momentarily. It was hard for Bubba to concentrate on anything but the loss of Lucy. His suffering had separated him from God. His grief had shut out His presence. His thoughts had blinded him from His light. And God waited patiently for Bubba to release himself from the material bonds that gripped his soul, so He could restore him to sanity.

Bubba wandered aimlessly across the countryside for many days before he finally fell on his knees one night and cried out for God.

The bright and shining light of God suddenly appeared before him. Bubba lifted his eyes toward the light that lit up the forest. He felt his grief slowly being lifted and the sorrow that had consumed him leave his thoughts as the holy light passed through his body. He then heard the voice of God and felt His spirit being restored within him. He felt relief as all ungodly thoughts were lifted from him. In a blink of an eye, God had restored him to sanity.

"You have suffered enough," said God. "Suffer no more. Both Lucy and Anna now abide with me."

"That is of great comfort to hear," uttered Bubba.

"Seldom do I play doorman," said God, "but I couldn't resist personally opening the gates of Heaven for Lucy. I sent a beautiful yellow dove to escort her into the Heavens. Hers was a very unselfish act that rarely happens in my kingdom. It really made my day."

"And you, Lord, hath made my day. I was very close

to insanity."

"Loss is often the factor that determines the value of love," said God.

"I am pleased you have paid me a visit after so long."

"The kingdom time is different from the earth time. If my timing is correct, we spoke only a few days ago. You were complaining about the lumps on your head. Your head looked like a goose had laid its eggs there."

Bubba smiled and rubbed the top of his head where the lump once stood. "If I ever told anyone you were funny they would certainly think I was crazy."

"You mortals take everything so seriously," said God. "Your life on earth passes quicker than a blink of an eye compared to life eternal. I wish I could hear more laughter down there. That would also make my day."

"And I now see that you are still troubled by something," said God, "and have some questions."

"Yes," Lord, replied Bubba." I have questions that burden me."

"You are certainly talking to someone with all the right answers. If I can't answer your question, no one can," God said with a chuckle.

"I have tried to serve you well and tragedy befalls me, yet many deny you and live long prosperous lives."

"And you wonder why bad things happen to good people?"

"Yes, Lord."

"Hear this, Bubba, so you will know and teach others. The sun shines on the just as well as the unjust. That is natural law. If a mule kicks you, Bubba, what shall you have learned?"

"Don't stand behind the mule."

"Exactly. And if you step in front of a speeding chariot what shall you expect?"

"To be ran over," answered Bubba.

"Precisely," replied the Lord. "Now I ask you, Bubba, when millions of my children die each day by unnatural death, which ones should I choose to live or to die when I love them all just the same?

"I now understand, Lord."

"Many expire before their time because of bad judgment and being at the wrong place at the wrong time, but once a mortal decides to do my will, they begin to use divine judgment which greatly eliminates the risk of early retirement on earth. Mortal man will always be subject to natural law and the indignities of unjust consequences. That is not my will but the will of natural law, poor judgment, and the exercise of free will. I want all my children to have a long beautiful life. That is my wish. I get very stressed out when I see good people make bad choices. Yes, I have all power over life and death but if I would intervene, it would negate the gift of free will to my children."

"But you saved me and Tonka from the sea. I do not understand why you could not save those in my family," said Bubba.

"Only in rare circumstances do I interfere with natural law," said God, "and only when it serves a very high purpose to all mankind. The angels in Heaven I have given the responsibility of overseeing individuals of promise but they are limited in their power. They can direct you to the market but it is up to you to choose the cut of beef you desire. And did it ever occur to you that you were saved to fulfill a divine mission?"

"How may I serve you?" asked Bubba

"First there are questions I must ask."

"But you already know the answers, Lord."

"Yes, Bubba, but I love it when my children do the talking for me. It pleases me to hear them say what I am thinking and already know. Tell me about your relationship with Lucy and what you learned."

"She was unlike me."

"That is why I created women different from men, so each may learn from the other."

"How well I know, Lord. Lucy liked apples while I preferred figs, and she liked the sunset while I preferred the sunrise, and then there was the market. I detested it and she loved it."

"And what did you do?"

"I learned to eat apples, get up late, and go shopping at the market."

"That is called compromise and not a very good one, but, nevertheless, a compromise. You have my complete attention, Bubba. Don't stop now."

"I learned a person, especially a woman, cannot be held against their will. They must have the freedom to make their own choices."

"How did you solve this with Lucy," asked God?

"I cut her loose after I had bonded her and gave her freedom."

"What else did you learn?"

"I gave her pearls to bribe her but she only wanted more pearls and not me. I could not buy her love. Those were very difficult days. It took me three lumps to come to my senses."

"How did you win her over?"

"I gave without expecting anything in return. She accepted me only after we had become friends. That was the real beginning of our life together."

"What was the bond that kept you and Lucy together?"

"You, Lord. Once we prayed together our entire life changed for the better. We often disagreed but seldom argued."

"As the saying goes," replied God, "people that pray together, stay together. The eternal bond between a man and a woman takes place when they become united as one in my spirit."

"Lucy became a different person, Lord."

"And so did you, Bubba. You learned the true meaning of love. Hear this Bubba, and chisel this one on stone. No greater love has a person than to lay down their life for another. Lucy gave up her life so you may live. Few are ever loved to that extent. You suffered great losses but have gained more than most mortals in my domain could ever hope for."

"My seven favorite requirements for a lasting relationship," continued God, "are unselfishness, compromise, freedom, friendship, trust, prayer, and love. Both you and Lucy magnificently displayed these principles in your relationship, and with you I am again well pleased."

"But my children, Lord. I don't think they fully understood my teaching. I worry about them as we speak."

"A parent can only lead his or her children by being an example. And you were a good example. And neither can a parent scorn a child for something they are doing themselves You did the very best that you could do, and that is all a parent can do but hope for the best."

"What now am I to do, Lord?

"What is it that you would like to do, Bubba?"

"To further serve you, and to one day be part of your kingdom."

"You certainly have all the right answers," replied God.

"Please show me the way, Lord. My will is your will."

"You shall now enter the final stage of your development. I shall send you on a journey, to a place called Alabama, and there, Bubba, you shall search for truth and when you shall find it, we shall talk again. And with those words the great light of God faded, and on the eleventh day God created Alabama.

When He saw what He had done, He was very amused and went about His business.

Bubba awoke from his transit sleep to find himself floating but also traveling with great speed through a large space where he felt himself move through many tunnels full of bright, colorful lights. He felt the sensation he had arms and legs but when he touched himself he realized he had no physical body. At first he thought he was dreaming, but everything he saw, smelled, heard, and touched seemed real. He heard the language of a thousand different cultures and briefly understood each one of them. He traveled through the Heavens, the sun, the moon and through a Universe so vast he understood the concept of time and space. He felt the warmth of the sun and the coldness of the moon. He touched the moon he had once tried to grab as he moved through it with great ease.

He saw the earth surrounded by a circular sea of beautiful crystal glass with thousands of dimensions and millions of pulsating colors. He witnessed spirits like himself moving freely through the Heavens.

He found himself moving through a large battlefield with weapons he had never seen, and ships with large guns the size of tree trunks that killed hundreds at a time. He felt the anguish of the dying men and saw thousands dead all over the world. He witnessed thousands dying from hunger and thirst and living on impoverished land and others dying from disease, and he briefly felt their pain and suffering. He recognized vast empires where one ruled over thousands and where man was pitted against man and fought until death. He saw many crying out for God, amid cruelty, death and destruction.

He witnessed a man carrying a cross for all the suffering of the world, and knew this was the Son of God, bearing the burdens of the world on his shoulders. He saw over a thousand years of civilizations pass quickly before him but understood each one.

After Bubba had seen this and much more, he found himself slowly descending inside of what looked like a large arena. Below he saw what appeared to be many strangely dressed warriors running from one end of a grassy field to the other with a coconut. He observed the warriors run, kick, throw and fight over the coconut, while thousands of spectators shouted, "Go, Alabama." He knew now he had reached his destination.

Bubba stood briefly in the middle of the arena until the warriors began running toward him. For a moment he was motionless as the warriors ran right through him with ease. He quickly discovered that with one single thought he could propel himself freely through solid matter and travel wherever he wanted to go. He enjoyed this newfound freedom and moved at will from one place to another.

He observed people of all different shapes, sizes, and colors. Some had teeth like his, some had many teeth, and some had no teeth at all. Many, he noticed, wore small glass objects covering their eyes, and some wore what looked like to Bubba to be small dark sea shells covering their ears and making music. Many of the men he observed looked like the women. Some of the men had long hair with pierced ears and noses, and many had arms and even their chests painted with drawings. He thought most of the spectators to be intoxicated with wine or crazy, shouting and swearing at the warriors on the field. He noticed many had small, white stems hanging from their lips producing fire and smoke, and he was very puzzled by this custom called cigarettes.

He marveled at the small yellow corn that was put inside a glass box that turned into large stones with jagged edges. He wondered why so many enjoyed eating these stones. He heard the words: *hot dogs, popcorn, peanuts,* and *football*. Before leaving the arena he understood the language of the spectators.

Outside were thousands of chariots without horses, painted in many different colors. Some roared like lions, moving about with the speed of a hawk, leaving trails of smoke. Some had eyes the size of saucers that lit up the sky.

In another arena, more chariots were going around in circles with no apparent destination while thousands of creatures shouted and screamed. A large sign in the center of the circle proclaimed, "NASCAR."

Wandering into a building with floors made of wood warriors as tall as small trees ran back and forth with another coconut, bouncing it up and down and throwing it at a fish net against a small wall. When the coconut sank into the fishnet, Bubba found it hard to understand why hundreds were rejoicing and others were swearing. The spectators called this *basketball*.

In another arena he found thousands of similar

creatures watching warriors hit the coconut with a stick. When a coconut was hit with the stick, he observed, the other warriors would try to catch the coconut and then hit the warrior with it as he ran around the area in an apparent circle. Spectators called it *baseball*.

Bubba wondered why this coconut was so important that thousands would sit for hours and watch it. Everywhere he went warriors were bouncing, kicking, throwing, or hitting a coconut. When he returned home, he thought to himself, he would certainly examine a coconut more thoroughly.

As Bubba moved freely about Alabama, he saw roads the size of great rivers and chariots speeding, day and night. The chariots gave way to the sound of a thousand trumpets, occasionally crashing into one another.

He observed tall temples with thousands of eyes that blinked like bats and giant towers rising into the clouds with fire and smoke, turning the sky black and changing the rivers into the color of blood. The local people called these monstrosities *skyscrapers*.

He saw creatures small and large dressed like lions and tigers with strange masks covering their faces. Small children dressed liked witches and demons begged for food outside homes while their parents stood nearby and laughed. He heard one call this strange custom *Halloween*.

There was no sense of time. Seasons changed in a blink of an eye, and he watched creatures cut good trees and take them inside their homes and worship them. They went to indoor markets where many shopped and bought gifts for the tree and decorated and dressed the tree with tiny fires that blinked on and off. He was amazed the creatures worshiped the tree for only a short period of time and then dragged the trees outside and threw them away.

He observed large men dressed in red with long white hair and beards, saying, 'Merry Christmas." He saw pictures and carvings of reindeer pulling a chariot through the sky. He heard creatures calling this person Santa Claus and saw small children writing letters to this funny-looking man and asking for gifts. Some children had many expensive gifts while some wept because they received no gifts. He soon understood it was a holy celebration, the birthday of God's son, and wondered what was holy about this custom.

Bubba witnessed thousands of men and women, caged like wild animals and trapped into small cages. It was a place of misery and sorrow, like the dungeons in Canna. He heard words like *lawyers, motions, appeals, parole,* and words he didn't understand, but he still felt their sorrow and plight.

Many things reminded him of Canna. They were both the wealthy and the poor. Some had castles while some had no place to sleep at night. He spent many days and nights in the homes of these people. He studied the devices necessary to their survival, and observed that many families were segregated, each to their own room, and relied upon things called microwaves, refrigerators, CD players, computers, cell phones and more devices he didn't understand. He observed the computer but could not figure out why these items were essential in almost every household. Many of the homes, he observed, had one computer for the adults and one for the children. He heard terms like *online, e-mail, hard drives,* and *software* and tried to understand the language out of curiosity, although he guessed this strange machine had nothing to do with truth.

The one thing that confused Bubba the most was a

gadget he called the magic box until he heard it called *television*. Inside this magic box were small creatures trapped inside. He wondered how they got there and why the families spent most of their time observing these smaller creatures. The small creatures would laugh and cry and the people outside the magic box would often do the same. He understood the coconut was called a ball and many of the little creatures trapped inside the magic box played with the ball just like they had in the arenas. It was mostly the men, he observed, that enjoyed watching the ball while the females often got mad because the men paid more attention to the warriors than to their wives.

Bubba followed one family away from the small magic box and into a large room full of people where he saw larger creatures trapped inside of a bigger box. He wondered if the creatures inside the boxes had a choice to be large or small. Before leaving he heard someone call the big box a *movie theater*.

Bubba was very confused but marveled at such things. He wondered why God had sent him to a place far less advanced than his own to find truth . . . this place called Alabama, where there was little order to anything and most creatures spent their lives sitting in front of this magic wooden box or looking at the machine they called a computer.

Bubba soon found what most creatures in Alabama called *church*. Others were called *synagogues, monasteries* and *cathedrals*. He was very excited when he heard God could be found in any number of these places. At last, he thought to himself, he was on the right path, and felt certain his mission would soon be complete.

He heard the word *Sunday*, and soon understood God only revealed himself to the people in Alabama on this particular day. He followed one family to this place called church. The family bickered and fought inside their speeding chariot because one of the children had made them late for church. Bubba thought this very odd. However late they were, Bubba thought, God would still be there when they arrived.

After observing many worshipers on Sunday he discovered almost everyone in Alabama was concerned about being late for church. Bubba decided he didn't want to be late for church either, and in a split second was inside a church that they called the *House of the Lord*. He floated around the church for most of the service waiting for God, often looking out the church windows for Him.

He heard the words *repent, hell, salvation, sin*, and realized the people inside the church had to obey many of the words before they could talk to God or have His blessings. He wondered why everyone had to gather inside the church when one could simply go to the nearest cliff or private place and talk with God. Many of these churches he found talked about a great big pit full of fire called hell where God gathers the creatures who are bad and burns them alive. This was very confusing to Bubba. God to him was beautiful, wonderful and full of love. He couldn't imagine God would create people in His image, and then burn them if they were bad. To Bubba, God was a creator, not a destroyer.

Bubba listened to one creature called a *preacher*. He held a book high in one hand and aimed a stubby finger right at many of the ones he thought had been bad. In the same breath, the preacher asked them for money, and many people were upset and crying. Bubba observed the creatures that cried the most gave the most money. Bubba thought it hard to give money to anyone who told him he was a bad person. If they wanted his money, he thought, they had better talk very good about him.

Bubba found a similar scenario in many of the churches he visited. Most preachers said God would be coming any day and they had to be ready for Him. Bubba rationalized if God hadn't arrived by now he just wasn't coming. And furthermore, he thought, the chances of catching God only between the hours of eleven and twelve on Sunday were very slim.

Most churches he observed based their belief on a book called *The Bible*. They called it the written word of God. This thing called *The Bible* was very confusing to Bubba. He found each church had its own interpretation of the book and if it was indeed the word of God, he wondered why God would write anything so confusing. God was, to him, very simple and to the point, and would never write a book people couldn't understand although he understood the value of this book called *The Bible*. He gave no more thought to the book and moved to other churches.

In one church called mass, he found men dressed like High Elders in long white robes trimmed in silver and gold. They wore pointed hats with gold crowns and spoke of a higher authority that wasn't God. They had small wooden boxes where the bad creature could talk to the good creature in private. He found they talked about things forbidden outside the box called sins. Neither creature could see one another, which was confusing to Bubba. He wondered to whom the good creature dressed in black talked when he was bad. He was certain truth would never be found in a dark wooden chamber where people whispered secrets to a priest. He wondered why the bad person didn't simply step out of the dark box, walk outside, get on his knees and talk directly to God.

Bubba became very discouraged in his quest to find truth inside the churches. He visited one place called a mosque where grown men prayed to an empty wall while the women stood behind them and were not allowed to approach this magic wall. Before Bubba left the mosque he traveled behind the wall to see if anyone was there. When he found nothing but concrete and brick, he was more confused.

In another church were men dressed in black with braided hair who wore black saucers on their heads and talked about the wrath of God. They talked about sacrifices, floods, and plagues God had sent upon the earth to those who did evil. They did not believe God had a son who visited earth, and were still waiting for the right one to show up.

Bubba was perplexed why God had sent him to Alabama, where creatures only devoted one day a week to gather and worship God and looked in all the wrong places for Him. The God he knew was one of love and not fear. Bubba couldn't imagine how anyone could fear God, when God was such a good friend . . . the One who truly loved everyone.

All the places he visited asked their worshipers for money to "keep the church alive" and he wondered how a church could be dying. In one home he visited on Sunday, a preacher was on every channel on the magic box, asking for money.

Bubba was having doubts about finding truth in Alabama. He felt he had failed God. The only truth he found in Alabama, he surmised, was their misconception of the living God. Perhaps that was the truth he was sent to find. He was too confused to think anymore.

Bubba found a place away from people and churches.

He needed a place of solitude, somewhere to ponder all of what he had seen and heard. He quickly found himself in a field of green, dotted with yellow and purple flowers that stretched into a large pasture where cattle and horses grazed leisurely, and some rested with their bellies turned toward the afternoon sun. Beyond the field he could see a few scattered houses and in the distance a peaceful sky with puffy white clouds against a sky of blue that stood still from the wind. In the center of the pasture was a large lake surrounded by pine trees and mossy oak trees with crooked limbs dipping into the lake.

Bubba rested his spirit beneath a large live oak and marveled at the tall trees with brown needles nestled in their tops and yellow flowers with solid black dots in the center.

Across the lake a small thin man well up in age pushed a grocery cart full of discarded aluminum cans. Bubba watched the old man stop momentarily and wipe the sweat from his brow and continue along the edge of the lake. At the opposite end of the lake was a small cove with a wooden dock over the water. There were a half dozen young children playing in the water and jumping off the dock onto a rubber raft.

He watched the children laugh and play in the lake. They reminded him of his own children when they were young, and he thought about the summer days with his children on Bali. He thought about Lucy and how much he missed her. He had come to terms with her death, but only by the grace of God. He just wished he could have spoken to her before she died and told her how much he loved her. But as suddenly as the wind and tides had swept Anna out to sea, Lucy was gone without a trace or a goodbye.

He thought about how circumstances on earth could

change so quickly and turn a life around for the better or the worse in a split second. Life, he thought, was so unpredictable, and perhaps, that was the beauty of it all; each day was an adventure into the unknown.

But he was at peace with himself over the death of both Lucy and Anna. He thought about how fortunate he was to have known and shared a part of his earthly life with them, and realized, resting under the oak tree, it was not what God takes but what God gives. He wondered if this was one of the truths he was sent to Alabama to find. He was certain it must be. He had shared a wonderful life with Lucy and those memories would live and burn like a soft ember inside his heart forever. He realized life on earth was but a temporary existence. Death was just an inevitable part of living and growing.

He thought about his children and silently asked God to protect and watch over them while he was in Alabama. He loved and missed them dearly and hoped they could find peace within themselves from the sorrow of their mother's death. He had forgiven the king and hoped his children would do the same.

Bubba was thinking about this and other things when he heard screams from the other end of the lake. A young girl about five years old had jumped off the dock and had not surfaced. He watched as the other children screamed and frantically jumped into the lake in an attempt to find her. Panic consumed the children. A couple of young boys ran to find the parents of the child while the others kept searching.

Bubba grieved silently for the girl. His own daughter had succumbed to a similar fate, and Bubba felt the sorrow that was to befall the parents. Bubba turned his spirit toward Heaven and called upon God to give him the strength to somehow save the girl. After speaking to God, he was turned to flesh. He stood and walked toward the girl. The children watched Bubba walk across the water toward the dock. One boy shouted, "Look, he's walking on water."

The children fell silent as they watched in awe as this strange man came out of nowhere, walked on water and suddenly disappeared into the lake.

The girl's lifeless body lay on the rocky bottom of the lake. Bubba reached out and took the girl by the hand, bringing her to the surface. He cradled her into his arms and walked across the water to a comfortable spot on land and laid the girl down. She had a deep gash on her forehead. Bubba touched her face gently with his hand and raised her chin up so he could see her face. When he touched the cut on the girl's head, it disappeared and the girl opened her eyes, smiling at Bubba. The girl asked, "Are you an angel?"

Bubba smiled at the girl, then noticed that the old man pushing the cart was standing just a few feet away. The man smiled at Bubba and gave an approving nod. Bubba returned the smile and then suddenly disappeared, turning back into a spirit.

In a few minutes the girl's panic-stricken parents were at the lake, surprised and happy their daughter was safe. The children explained to the parents a strange man had walked on the water and rescued their friend. The parents were skeptical of their story, and soon a rescue unit and the police were searching the lake for the man's body. They assumed he had drowned while trying to save the girl. When the body could not be found, the children were questioned one by one, and they all told the same story in detail. They explained it was a tall man with dark hair and eyes that walked on top of the water with a limp and had a gentle smile. When the police asked the girl, who had saved her, she simply, replied, "An angel."

Soon the press was on the scene, and the daily newspaper read, "Angel Saves Young Girl from Drowning." Another read, "City Searches for Angel."

The following day thousands gathered at the lake in hopes of catching a glimpse of the angel. The incident made national news. Local merchants and retailers capitalized on the incident. Many sold water from the lake labeled as "holy water" while others sold T-shirts, key chains, and souvenirs with angel designs. Some merchants claimed the angel had visited their store; dozens claimed they had actually seen the angel walking in the woods or along some desolate stretch of highway. As the rumors of angel sightings grew so did the crowds. The country roads leading into the small town were jammed with traffic, and extra police had to be called to duty.

At the lake, congregations from various faiths gathered to pray, sing, and be part of the miracle. One man stood perched on a boat dock with his bible in hand, proclaiming the end of the world. A group of women showed up with signs protesting abortion; another group displayed signs advocating women's rights. Every cause, it seemed, had a sign somewhere for or against something.

In a couple of days the quite-serene pasture quickly turned into a media phenomenon and angels' sightings spread from Alabama across the nation. Every car or truck on a dirt road seemed to leave a trail of dust that formed an apparition of an angel. Downtown lunch breaks in many cities were spent pointing toward the sky, watching the clouds form an assortment of celestial host with each gust of wind. One woman called into a local radio station to report that after praying and during dinner, she saw an apparition of the Virgin Mary in her mashed potatoes. Apparitions were reported on garage doors, lawns, sidewalks, windshields, and even on milk cartons.

The children were invited to appear on a national talk show and some received calls from Hollywood agents who wanted to make a movie deal.

Bubba watched all these events unfold and realized the people in Alabama were just as lost as he. He knew his journey was coming close to an end even though he wasn't sure just how long he had been in Alabama. His journey had been like a dream with the days and nights blending together with no conception of normal time.

It had been a fascinating experience, one he would never be able to fully explain to anyone. He had watched the chariots at feeding time — the driver opening the chariots mouth, removing a long thin stick, studying it, emptying a strange solution inside the hungry beast, and then closing its mouth until it was fed again. The chariot would then roar like a lion and its stomach would growl with the sound of music. How could he explain this to anyone in Canna? Or the giant silver bird that soared through the sky without flapping its wings? Or the people inside the magic box?

My family would certainly have me committed to the dungeons for the afflicted, Bubba thought, if he spoke of the physical trapping of this place called Alabama. There were many things he would keep to himself when he returned to Canna, especially the incident at the lake where he had gone to meditate and pray, and where his solitude was interrupted by his physical appearance in the flesh . . . and the chain of events that followed. But he was happy he had gone to the lake for the sake of the child and wondered how she was doing. In fact, none of the children had returned to the lake since the incident, and now something struck Bubba as very odd: neither had the old man. The very person who could collaborate the children's stories had left before the parents had arrived that afternoon. When everyone at the lake, it seemed, wanted their stories or pictures on the evening news, the man who actually saw Bubba in the flesh had disappeared. Bubba wondered why the man had not come forward to claim his moment of fame or perhaps a generous reward for his story.

Bubba's desire to find the old man who was pushing the cart was immediately fulfilled as Bubba found himself observing a mountain of discarded aluminum cans, used tires, refrigerators, copper tubing and an assortment of metals and junk in the man's back yard.

* * * * *

Henry Hackett was pushing eighty years old but had the zest and spunk of a man half his years. He claimed his good health came from walking ten to fifteen miles a day while collecting drink cans or delivering fresh baked bread and cakes to the homeless or needy.

Behind Henry's thick wire-rimmed glasses, his soft blue eyes always sparkled, and Henry was known for his cheerful disposition and warm smile. He enjoyed tipping his dress hat when greeting people, especially the ladies, showing off his crown of thick silver hair, and he often twirled the ends of his handlebar mustache with his fingertips while talking. It was not uncommon for Henry to stop a total stranger on the street and strike up a conversation.

The small suburban town of Weukeesaw, Alabama, had been Henry's home for the last forty years. He lived just outside the slums and inner-city projects of South Birmingham with his black-and-white mutt, Trevor, and his German cat, Spooky. His modest wood frame house was mostly like the others built in the fifties on the quite tree lined street: a wooden screened-in front porch, tin roofs, tall windows with a lot of panes, and a open single-car garage. Henry's house was in much need of painting and repairs, but more conspicuous were the year-round Christmas lights on the house and a set of lighted reindeer in the front yard. Henry liked the idea that his house was easy to find for new homeless people picking up fresh-baked bread.

Henry was pushing a cart full of collected cans and junk into his backyard when he heard Trevor barking. Behind his house was an old tin shed with an open front Henry used as a woodshop. There he would flatten the cans and weigh them for the recycling truck. Trevor had dashed into the shed as Henry approached and stood at the front, wondering what caused Trevor to bark. Trevor's bark turned to a howl, and his hair stood up straight on his back. Henry observed Trevor for a few moments with a curious eye, twirled his mustache, and said, "It must be you, I see."

Bubba wondered, *Can he really see me?*

"No, I can't see you," remarked, Henry, as if he had read Bubba's thoughts, "but Trevor sure knows you're there. Right boy?" He reached down and stroked Trevor, who wagged his tail, happy his master had found the intruder.

"My name is Henry and this is Trevor. Nothing gets past Trevor, not even you. But you're not the first spirit the good Lord has sent my way. That's why I didn't come back to the lake. Already been one reporter snooping around here and I don't need more. I don't think that's what the Lord wants, more nuts out there at the lake trying to get on television. And if I claimed I saw an angel, I'd be right up with there with the rest of them. But I'm sure glad the good Lord sent you there. I've already thanked him for sending you to save the child but the next time around," Henry said with a jest, "try to stay off the water. It sure stirred up an awful mess."

Henry removed his walking cane from the handlebar of the cart and started toward the house. Trevor followed behind Bubba, wagging his tail and sniffing the ground over which Bubba moved.

"You might as well come in for a spell. I'll give you the grand tour unless you gotta get back up there," he said, with a smile, lifting an eye upward.

"I'm sorry I couldn't back up the children's story but they'll be just fine without my comments."

Henry lifted himself up the step with the help of his cane. The rusty hinges on the screen door to the porch squeaked as he opened the door and stepped inside, letting the door slam behind him.

"Been meaning to replace those hinges one day."

Henry walked a few feet to another door, inserted a key, and walked inside with Trevor close behind.

"This is my kitchen," said Henry, turning his eyes as though Bubba was standing beside him.

The walls of an adjoining room had been removed to accommodate a larger kitchen, evident by the mismatched paint and dry-wall patches. In the center of the room was a large chopping block, and two shelved walls hosted a variety of baked goods. Henry pointed his cane to a large commercial oven. "That's my pride and joy there. I'm a retired baker, if you didn't know. I can bake over a hundred loaves of bread a day, that is, depending on a good recycling day."

Henry moved down the narrow hall of the house to the front room. His cat was asleep on the sofa when they entered. Spooky gave a loud hiss and dashed out of the room. He chuckled, "Now you see why I named her Spooky."

The room was cluttered with old newspapers and magazines. An oak grandfather clock stood in the corner, surrounded by antique furniture, thick oriental rugs, an aging sofa, a roll-top desk displaying an open Bible, and the smell of age hung in the air. Henry put his hat on a rack and walked to the entrance to an adjoining room, stopping briefly to point out a family picture on the wall. "That's me and my wife Anna, and our daughter Christina in my younger years. Christina was only twelve when the picture was taken." Henry lowered his eyes and paused. "About a year later, I lost both of them."

On the walls of the room were dozens of newspaper clippings attached with pins. Henry pointed his cane to one clipping. "That's Doctor Perez there. She just set up a practice in Weukeesaw. I saw her a couple of months ago to look at my spine. Charged me an arm and a leg for the checkup." Henry laughed. "If only she knew."

Henry pointed to another clipping with a picture of a black man. "That's George C. Padgett, there. He's now a big civil rights attorney. He used to be just a street thug in the projects when he was growing up. Stayed in trouble with the law, now he's thinking about running for mayor."

The conversation and clippings made little sense to Bubba, but he was intrigued by Henry. He was the first person in Alabama who had communicated directly with him. He felt certain Henry was part of the reason for his coming to Alabama but was confused as to how Henry might fit in his search for truth.

Henry turned toward Bubba, then shifted his eyes back to a stack of photo albums that were collecting dust in the corner of the room. "Those are more of my students over there. I've tried to keep track of their lives but after college it was hard."

Bubba followed Henry back into the front room where Trevor lay sprawled comfortably on the carpet. Henry walked to the television and turned it on. The picture was fuzzy, but a slight tap from Henry's cane caused the picture to clear. He then looked at his watch and took a seat in a rocking chair in front of the television and next to Trevor. Bubba hovered over Henry, watching the magic box, satisfied with Henry's answer and wondering if he should stay or go. Henry was just about to answer that question.

"The children will be on national television in a moment. I seldom watch TV, but I couldn't help but see what they have to say about you. Ain't nothing but bad news on anymore. No one likes to listen to good news these days, especially if it doesn't concern them. But you have about three minutes to make it to Chicago by four o'clock if you want to see the the children in person."

Trevor raised his head and ears to the sound of the screen door's rusty hinges opening and closing. Henry turned her eyes toward the back door and raised a curious eyebrow at Trevor, who came to his feet and stood alert. Rising from the rocking chair, Henry looked down the hallway toward the back door. It was then he heard the rumble of thunder in the skies. He turned and looked toward the front windows. A summer wind lifted the window sheers and the sound of raindrops bounced off the tin roof.

Henry walked to the front door, opened it, and looked out. He was greeted by a warm breeze on a hot June day. A gray rain cloud slowly covered a gold shadow cast by the sun across a hazy blue sky. A sudden burst of heavy rain beat down followed by a loud roar of thunder. Henry watched the rain, smiled, and thought to himself what a beautiful day it had been.

* * * * *

An attractive middle-aged black woman was beginning her opening dialog to the studio audience when Bubba arrived. "Today," she said, "we have some very special guests from Weukeesaw, Alabama. The children who started the angel craze that's now sweeping across American are here with their story. Thousands of angel sightings have been reported daily to television and radio stations across the country. I had a chance to talk to these children backstage, and if you don't believe in angels, you might after hearing their story. We also have some clergy here and a child psychologist, who says he can explain what really happened at the lake that afternoon. It's a rare phenomenon he calls collective stress disorder. But first let's give warm round of welcome to P.J., Kevin, Randy, and Kimberly."

The children entered and were seated on stage. Kimberly, who was saved from drowning sat closest to the host. After an adjustment with the children's microphones by a stage hand, the host looked at the audience with the mike in her hand and turned toward the children. "Okay, you kids say you saw an angel, and Kimberly was saved from drowning by an angel, correct?"

The children nodded in agreement.

"Who wants to begin?"

P.J., a black boy, eight years old, raised his hand. "Go ahead, P.J.," the host said.

"We were jumping on and off the dock, trying to land on the float. Then Kimberly jumped in and didn't come up."

Randy, a nine-year-old boy, continued, "When she didn't come up for a while we got worried and dove in after her but couldn't find her."

"How long was she missing?"

The children looked at one another for an answer.

Kevin, the oldest of the group at ten, finally spoke. "She was missing for about five minutes." The other children nodded in agreement.

"That's when you sent a couple more kids to Kimberly's house to get her parents, right?" the host asked, again receiving positive nods from the children.

"What happened next?"

"That's when the angel came and got me," said Kimberly.

P.J. said, "We were crying and scared when we looked on the lake and saw him walking toward us."

The host's face drew up in surprise. "He was walking on top of the water?"

Kevin replied, "Yeah, and he didn't even get his feet wet." The comment drew laughter from the audience.

"And all of you saw the angel?" the host asked. Again, a chorus of nodding heads showed unanimity.

"Did you kids get a good look at the angel?"

Randy said, "Yeah, he was sorta funny looking. He was old, and walked with a limp, like something was wrong with his leg."

P.J. noted, "He looked sorta dirty but he was smiling."

"And he needed a shave," Kimberly said.

The host turned toward the audience. "Wow, this isn't our normal perception of angels with white robes, flowing hair and beautiful wings. Here we have a handicapped angel that needs a bath."

The audience laughed, and the host turned back to the children. "Do all of you agree with the description?"

Again, the children nodded yes. Kimberly spoke up and said, "And he was missing a finger."

"He was missing a finger?"

"Yeah, when he pulled me out of the water, I was looking at his hand."

" Kimberly had a cut over her eye and he made it go away," P.J. offered.

"Is that right Kimberly?"

Kimberly put her finger to her head where the gash had been, showing the audience. "I had a cut right here before he touched me."

"After he pulled you from the water, did he say anything to you?" the host asked Kimberly.

"He just smiled and then left."

"Disappeared?"

"Yeah, just *poof* and left like a bird," said Kimberly.

The host made a serious face. "The medical examiners said they could find no evidence of a cut or abrasion on your forehead. They also found no water in your lungs. Are you children pulling our legs?"

Kimberly lifted her eyes directly at the host and made an equally serious face. "God doesn't like people that lie."

"Where did you learn that?" the host asked.

"I learned it in Sunday school."

"What religion are you, Kimberly?"

"Baptist."

"And you, P.J.?"

" Methodist."

"And you Kevin?"

"Catholic."

"And you, Randy?"

"Baptist."

"And all of you go to church on a regular basis?"

The children gave affirmative nods.

The host turned to the audience. "We have two Baptist, a Methodist, and a Catholic here who all attend church on a regular basis. What do you folks in the audience think happened? Did these kids really see an angel?"

The audience gave a loud positive applause.

The host smiled. "Well, there is another twist to the story. They say another person was at the lake who saw the angel."

"Henry was at the lake," said P.J.

"Who is Henry?" the host asked.

Kevin replied, "He brings us cup cakes all the time."

"Chocolate cup cakes," Kimberly added.

"And he likes to tell us funny jokes," said Randy.

"Well, we contacted one of our affiliates, in Birmingham, WBSA to see if they could locate Henry to verify the children's story, and Henry wasn't hard to find," the host said. "It seems he's somewhat of a local celebrity. Henry has been delivering fresh baked breads and cakes to the homeless and needy for over twenty years. Henry declined to comment on the incident, only to say, 'We should search our hearts for the truth.' But Henry left us with one clue to the mystery. Yes, he gave our reporter . . . you guessed it . . . a freshly baked angel food cake."

The audience broke out in wild applause.

The host asked, "Where do you children think the angel is now? Do you think you'll see him again?"

Kimberly answered, "He's right here watching us."

"Wow, he's right here in the studio?"

"Yeah, he'll always be my friend," said Kimberly.

"If you had one thing to say to our studio audience today what would it be?"

Kimberly smiled confidently. "You just gotta believe us and have faith."

The host turned to the studio audience and said, "'You just gotta believe us and have faith.' Those are pretty powerful words coming from a five-year-old. I think we've seen an angel right here on stage today, audience. What do you think?"

The audience again gave a loud positive applause, with many standing to clap.

Bubba was pleased he had come and listened to the children. He knew he would never see the young girl again but realized, in addition to saving her, he had made a difference in her life. For that reason alone, he was glad he had come to Alabama. Before leaving, he heard the words *The Oprah Winfrey Show.*

Bubba turned his spirit upward and asked God's permission to return. In a split second he was standing in the shining light of God, at the very spot his sojourn had begun.

"How was your journey?" asked God.

"With all respect, God, why did you send me to this place called Alabama where I did not find truth?"

"I chose Alabama at random," replied God. "I guess it began with an 'A,' but that is not important. Most mortals are just like the people who live in Alabama.

They have lost their way and no longer know truth. But the fact is, you did find truth in Alabama. You have yet to fully comprehend your mission.

"The mortals of the realm look for so-called miracles," continued God, "but fail to watch the sunrise and sunset, which are in themselves miracles. The birth of a child is a miracle. The microscopic world in which they live is a miracle, but few realize miracles take place every moment of their lives. It was important you have a look into the future so you may know these things and be wiser.

"Many in my kingdom call earth the world of the ball, or the coconut as you called it," continued God. "The warriors are given great wealth and fame because they are good and swift with the ball. Statues and artifacts are often displayed in their likenesses because they have conquered the ball. The warriors are called heroes by those who worship them. Healthy sports are very good and I have no indifference to these warriors or their sport, but many of my creatures pay more attention to these heroes than they do to me, their families . . . and more so, themselves. And the little creatures you saw inside the magic box are also worshiped as heroes and are given great wealth and fame. It is a worthy profession to those that make believe they are someone else. Harm is only done when they believe they are someone other than my creation. But most that worship them are more concerned about the lives of these heroes than their own lives.

"Every mortal must toil to survive," continued God. "That is part of the learning process. But each mortal has been given a special gift and how one discovers that gift and chooses an occupation is up to that individual. Unfortunately, many never realize this gift. They never search their hearts for something they enjoy doing but instead are concerned about the material benefits of the endeavor. Some are chores they feel have no meaning or purpose, but if they labor in the glory of the kingdom, they shall find their true purpose on earth."

Bubba held his hands before him, palms up. "I do not understand, Lord. In Alabama I searched very hard."

"Yes, Bubba, and you were more successful than you realize. I ask you, who saved the little girl in the lake?"

"You did, Lord."

"Yes, Bubba, belief that I would answer your prayer is just one of the truths you discovered in Alabama. Tell me, Bubba, when you asked for help, what happened?"

"I became a creature like myself once again and was able to rescue the girl."

"Yes, Bubba, and quote me on this one: 'He that knocks on my door, the door shall be opened. And he that asks it shall be given unto him.' Now I ask you, Bubba, what made you think I would come to your aid?"

"Because I believed and trusted in you, Lord. You once told me that you and only you had the power over life or death and I believed you."

"You are right again, Bubba. You believed in me and had faith that I would fulfill my promise."

"I do not understand this word *faith*, Lord."

"Faith is the belief in those things you cannot see or touch but know to be true, and in believing in me, your faith helped save the girl. I had Kimberly, the young girl say it for me, 'Believe and have faith,' yet many adults do not comprehend these simple truths said by a child. And yes, you saved her life, but never make the mistake, Bubba, like many of my creatures do. You have no power unless I give it unto you. My creatures are nothing but instruments and through them I work. It makes my job a lot easier than doing it myself. And now I ask you, Bubba, what is another great truth you found in Alabama?"

Bubba lowered his head and then slowly lifted his eyes toward God. "I do not know, Lord. I was very confused."

"Henry was a perfect example of a supreme truth, Bubba. He is one of my favorite creations. In the prime of Henry's life, he lost his wife and daughter in an car accident . . . chariots as you call them. It was a very difficult time for Henry. He blamed me for a long time, even cursed me. Then one day, Henry fell on his knees and cried out for my help. That was the beginning of our long friendship together. Henry received a sizable amount of money in a settlement from an insurance company. He invested the money and in a few years he had amassed a good fortune. Henry had never been able to afford a higher education for himself; therefore, after a lot of prayer and thought, he decided to set up a foundation for higher education for the poor and underprivileged. The pictures you saw on his walls were only a few of the hundreds he had helped. And all the while, remaining anonymous, he continues to give to his fellow brothers and sisters."

"I understand, Lord."

"Hear this Bubba. The real heroes in my kingdom often enter without name or number but because of their service to mankind. The desire to serve your fellow brother is the final step in the evolution of the human soul. It is the final result of practicing all the other truths. To serve not out of moral obligation, or guilty conscience, but to serve others with a joyful heart is the greatest gift a person can give to themselves and to one another."

"Should one give up everything, Lord?"

"That is a very good question, Bubba. Henry's

decision to live a modest life was of his own choosing. I do not expect my mortals to live in poverty. I wish all a prosperous life. It is by a person's heart that I judge. If a person truly seeks to do My will, material wealth and possessions become less important and that person will soon discover the gift of life is truly found in serving others. I wish there were more people like Henry."

"Many in the churches spoke your name, Lord. Were they all wrong in their belief?"

"Bubba, how many coconuts have you gathered on the seashore?"

"Many, Lord."

"And did they all look the same?"

"Yes, I couldn't tell one from the other."

"Did you know how much milk was in one as opposed to the other?"

"Only when I opened the coconut did I find the one with the most milk."

"There are as many beliefs," said God, "as coconuts on the seashore. Only by opening one's heart and looking within does one discover these truths. Some mortals, Bubba, could not recognize the truth if coconuts full of milk fell and bounced off their heads. They are spiritually stagnant and open only one coconut when there are many. They have been institutionalized by tradition and doctrine, and have become spiritually lazy. Truth is revelatory and constantly revealing itself for those who seek to do the divine will. Do you think the butterfly grew out of a moth by mistake? Do you think the snake sheds its skin by its own will? Do you think the beautiful oak grew from a small acorn by mistake? Through the bee I gave you honey and through the goat I gave you milk. Every blade of grass or grain of sand has a universe within a universe and breathes my spirit. Nothing on earth is by accident but a grand design by the Architects of Heaven. As on earth it is also in Heaven, where I have many that carry on my work and creations. But now I see something is bothering you."

"With all respect, Lord, it bothers me that you always know what I'm thinking."

"I know what *everyone* is thinking, so be careful what you think."

"I miss Tonka. I understand Lucy and Anna abide in your kingdom, but you failed to mention Tonka. Will I ever see him again?"

"I'll have to give that one some consideration. A resurrection request is a big order."

"But I believe you can do anything, Lord."

"I can do anything, Bubba. Miracles happen every day for those who sincerely seek to do my will."

"And what is my work on earth that I may fulfill it?" asked, Bubba.

"The Fatherhood of God and the Brotherhood of Man, Bubba. That is my will for mankind on earth. A person cannot claim to love me and hate his brother nor can a person claim to love his brother and deny me. Those two truths go hand in hand, like the coconut and the tree. One could not exist without the other. Sincere love and prayer will open the gates to the heart and truth therein will be found. My mortals look for me up here when I am in reality down there. I like being inside more than outside. That's why I dwell inside all my mortals. I'm always constantly amazed they are searching for me outside of themselves and never think of looking inside to find me.

"No mortal, continued God, "will ever know absolute truth. Each great religion was founded by a small element of truth but there are many pathways into my house, and no particular religion holds all the keys to the kingdom. Truth, like everlasting life, is an individual choice. Once a creature decides to do my will, he becomes a new creature and all that is old passes away and new truths are discovered each day. In Alabama you discovered seven of my favorite spiritual truths, Bubba. They are faith, belief, trust, prayer, service, worship, and love. Those seven covenants are the pathway into my kingdom."

"What shall I do with these covenants, God?"

"You have united body, mind, and spirit in your journey on earth, Bubba. With you I am well pleased. I invest in you the power to do whatever you would like to do, and seldom do I go out on a limb, but you, Bubba, I know will not let me down."

"But Lord, I am only one man and very old."

"One day Bubba, I will send a son unto the world to explain these things, and He will also be but one man among many, but his words and good deeds will live in the hearts of men forever. One cannot light a candle under a bushel for any length of time before its light begins to shine. So go forth and teach others what you have learned."

"Where shall I begin?"

"Return to Canna. Your many children and grandchildren miss you. Teach first the young ones because their hearts are not tarnished by time, and if just one comes to believe in my word, you have changed the world for a better place to live. I must go now."

"But I am afraid, Lord. Most will not believe what I have seen and heard. They will only think that I am feeble."

"I understand your fears, Bubba. But speak only of certain things I have revealed to you. Truth is never ready for all people at all times. Your faith will give you the right answers when the time comes. You will be ridiculed for your teaching by many, but remember I will be by your side for now and until the end of time. My pleasure is found in those I create who choose to do the divine will and make the world a better place to live. You have proven yourself far beyond my expectations. Now and forever the angels of Heaven will be by your side. Now peace be unto you."

When the great and radiant light of God faded, Bubba was renewed with great strength and spiritual insight. He raised his arms toward Heaven and praised God. When he had finished giving praise to God, he began his journey back to Canna. He found a staff to help him walk, and with Gork leading the way, he soon walked into the gates of the city.

His hair was long and white, his clothes dirty and tattered, and his sandals were worn thin. He was tired from the long walk. Just inside the city he stopped at the seashore and rested, taking a seat in the busy marketplace. The city was bustling with activity. He watched the hundreds of people that crowded the streets of the market, shopping and selling their wares. He gripped his staff and tried to stand but was too tired, thirsty, and hungry. He couldn't remember the last time he or Gork had eaten. Soon a group of children were standing in front of him. One pointed at Bubba and laughed at his appearance. Another picked up a small stone and tossed it at him. Now all five children were jeering and tossing pebbles at Bubba. Bubba said nothing. He just smiled at the children. A small crowd quickly gathered, watching the children. An older lady in the crowd pointed at Bubba's feet. "He is a leper," she whispered to the others. Now a shopkeeper approached.

He was middle-aged, short and stout with a belly that stood over his waistline.

"You must leave," he shouted. "You cannot beg in front of my store."

"I am here to see the princess," exclaimed Bubba.

The storekeeper laughed, putting his hands on his hips. "And who are you to ask for the princess?"

Bubba raised his soft eyes at the storekeeper. "I am her father," he replied. "Go tell Princess Zia her father is here."

The storekeeper studied Bubba for a moment then realized Bubba's gentle eyes and soft smile spoke the truth. He clasped his hands together, walking closer to Bubba. The crowd covered their mouths in awe and stood silently.

"You must forgive me and my children," begged the storekeeper.

"You need not ask forgiveness. I am thirsty and need only a cup of water," replied Bubba.

The storekeeper turned to the young boys, raising his hand at one, about to strike him. "I shall punish the children well," said the storekeeper.

"Do not strike the child," said Bubba. "They are only young and foolish."

A woman knelt before Bubba with a cup of water. Bubba took the cup of water and after having a drink looked at the woman and thanked her.

"He is my husband and two of the boys are my children," said the woman. "I beg you not to tell the princess of this matter. She will certainly have us flogged."

"I shall say nothing," said Bubba. "Only tell the princess her father is waiting."

The woman nodded and hurried away.

* * * * *

While Bubba waited, he thought about his journey to Alabama. He lifted his eyes toward the afternoon sun and watched the clouds drift while thinking about all he had seen and done, and wondered how long he had been gone. In a moment of spiritual clarity, he was overwhelmed by a divine revelation that prompted him to stand and point his staff toward Heaven.

He laughed aloud, "What a marvelous journey, considering perhaps I never left Canna."

Bubba sat back down, nodding his head, smiling to himself like he had just discovered a great truth, and perhaps he had. He remembered when God sent him to Alabama, the sun stood directly overhead, and Gork was perched on a tree limbs a few feet away. When he returned he was on his knees in the same position as when he left, Gork was still perched on the same limb, and the noon sun stood directly overhead.

Bubba laughed aloud, nodding his head and smiling toward the Heaven. The full impact of his journey was just unfolding before him, all engineered by the miraculous imagination of God.

His journey to Alabama: the magic box, the churches, the chariots, Henry Hackett, Kimberly, the talk show. . . was it nothing but a play staged in his mind and hosted by the All-mighty God? Bubba would never know. But if so, it would have made the trip just that much more spectacular.

The royal carriage arrived that afternoon to pick up Bubba. The princess had taken the carriage instead of the coach. The coach was closed in while the carriage had no top. It was a bright fall day, the air was crisp and cool, and the topless carriage was fitting for the ride. As it slowly made its way through the crowded streets of Canna, the citizens bowed as it passed. The princess rarely traveled to the marketplace, and the presence of the royal carriage, drawn by seven white Arabian horses, was seldom seen by the working-class Canites except on special occasions.

Zia stopped at the homes of Makia and Celeste so they might ride with her to pick up their father and discuss what they should do with him. He had been missing for close to a month and they feared the worst. The last they remembered was the billowing smoke from his home he had vowed he would always keep. Their father was, they guessed, at least eighty years of age, but there was no way they could document his age since he had no parents. He had always told his children he and Lucy had just appeared, born from the Heavens and had fallen upon the earth as simply as a raindrop. The existence of their mother and father would always remain a mystery to them.

Unlike the early years, the three sisters did not meet often and relished any occasion they could get together, away from their husbands, to gossip and be themselves and sisters. The ride to pick up their father had given them a chance to talk. They were still mourning the death of their mother. They all agreed there would never be a closure. The fact she had been beheaded was too painful for the sisters to discuss. Their hearts were full of hate and they could only think of ways to avenge her death.

Before they reached their destination, Makia saw their father walking alongside the road toward the carriage.

"Look, Zia, it is Father," Makia said, pointing her finger in the direction of the road ahead.

Zia and Celeste raised themselves up to the edge of the seat to get a better look but could not see him. Zia put her hand over her eyes to block the sun, squinting.

"Where, Makia? Are you sure it was Father?"

Makia laughed. "How many old men walk the streets with a hawk on their shoulder?"

The many pedestrians and pack mules blocked their view, but as the carriage slowly made it way through the street, the crowds stepped aside and within moments Bubba was standing directly in front of the carriage.

Zia tapped the driver on the shoulder and instructed him to stop alongside their father.

"Where do you think you are going, Father," asked Zia.

"Anywhere but here, Zia."

"It is a long walk to the palace," exclaimed Celeste.

Bubba let out a hearty laugh. "You children think that your father is not used to walking. If I waited any longer on my daughters, the sun would be coming up."

"I am sorry I am late," explained, Zia. "I have been

very busy."

"You are the busiest woman in the world, Zia, to have nothing accomplished at the end of the day."

Makia and Celeste burst into laughter.

The sisters always enjoyed their father's honesty and humor and were very pleased to see him.

Zia opened the carriage door. "Are you just going to stand there or get into the carriage?"

Eli stepped down from the carriage and walked around to assist Bubba. Bubba handed Eli his staff. Eli leaned the staff against the carriage and took Bubba by the arm and helped him into the carriage.

Bubba took a seat next to Zia, facing Makia and Celeste. Gork fluttered his wings, a sign he made when he was happy.

"Gork is very happy to see his family," said Bubba. "And all my daughters are as beautiful as the day they were born."

Makia raised her hand out for Gork. Gork quickly stepped onto her hand as the carriage pulled away.

"I see Gork still remembered me," said Makia

"Gork never forgets anyone," replied Bubba.

Celeste now held out her hand. Gork stepped onto the back of her hand, fluttering his wings.

"My fondest memories as a child was playing with Gork and, of course, Tonka," said Celeste.

Zia interrupted saying, "We have been very worried about you, Father. We didn't know what happened to you after Mother's death."

"We are pleased you are alive," added Celeste.

"Where have you been?" asked Makia.

"I have been to a place called Alabama," said Bubba.

"Where is this place?" asked Zia. "I have never heard of it."

"It is very far away," replied Bubba.

"And how did you get there, Father?" asked Makia.

"I flew," replied Bubba. "Like the birds of Heaven. It was a marvelous journey."

The sisters looked at one another. They all silently agreed, nodding their heads at one another, their father was feeble and had lost his mind since the death of their mother.

Zia put her hand over her father's. "We will take care of you from here on, Father."

"You are welcome to stay in my home," said Celeste.

"And mine also," added Makia.

"I am very thankful I have a beautiful family that loves me," said Bubba. "But I shall rebuild my home just like it was and there I will stay."

"We are afraid you may fly off again to Alabama," said Zia with a chuckle.

"I have seen enough of Alabama," said Bubba. "And besides, my wings are very tired."

"Now we have a father who has sprouted wings," laughed Makia.

"And one who thinks he can fly," added Celeste.

The sisters all burst into laughter.

Bubba raised his arms and moved back and forth like he was soaring through the air.

"Stop it, Father," said Zia, still laughing. "You are too much to behold."

* * * * *

The grand palace stood high up on the hill, but just below the king's castle. It was five stories high, made of marble and stone. Below each of the many tall windows was a half-moon shaped stone balcony with iron railings. The four corners of the palace had round pillars that towered above the roof line and also served as watchtowers. The grounds surrounding the palace were magnificently landscaped with scrubs, flowers and hundreds of rose bushes. There were seven gardens in all, connected by stone walkways that branched off from a central fountain fed by an underground spring. In the center stood a towering marble statue of Zia. Dante had overseen the construction of the palace, having designed it himself. He was very proud of his accomplishment and took pride in showing it off.

Zia took her sisters home. Celeste asked her father to let her children keep Gork for the night and Bubba agreed, knowing Gork loved to play with small children.

Bubba had never visited the palace. He eyes traveled the palace grounds as the carriage made its way past the gated entrance where a guard stood and saluted. Bubba was not impressed but more amused that Dante and Zia had devoted so much of their wealth and time into something that could only feed their egos. But he dared not say anything negative that would spoil his visit. He was happy his children were doing well regardless of how misguided he thought they were.

Dante walked down the steps and opened the carriage door for Bubba. "Welcome to our home, I am pleased you are doing well."

"And you, Dante," Bubba said, lifting his eyes toward the palace. "I am glad you are doing well, perhaps much too well."

Dante laughed.

"My father has never lost his sense of humor," laughed Zia. "He said God told him his first joke, and he has been laughing ever since. You two have never really talked at length during all these years. It should be a most interesting evening."

"Where are Gabriel and my other grandchildren?" asked Bubba as Dante and Zia helped him up the steps, each holding one of his arms.

"Gabriel is at the theater for the night, and the children are staying with friends. We did not expect you tonight; otherwise they would have been here."

"We were concerned about you," added Dante.

"Father says that he has been on a long trip to a place called Alabama."

"I would enjoy hearing about your trip. I'll have one of my men chart it on the map. The name is new to me."

Bubba stopped just before entering and turned to Dante. "Unless your men have wings, it's going to be very hard to find."

Dante laughed. "Please come inside."

The palace floors were solid white marble with highly polished stone pillars reaching to a cathedral ceiling decorated with fine art and hand-carved gold and silver ornaments. There were more than fifty chambers inside, lavishly furnished with fine drapes and exquisite furniture made of birch and mahogany. The centerpiece of the palace was an indoor pool with a waterfall two stories high that poured down into the pool.

"Zi and Michael, your two sons, and the family will be here tonight for a welcome home dinner," said Zia.

Bubba stopped and turned to Zia with an eyebrow raised.

"I need not be reminded Zi and Michael are my sons. I understand you think your father is feeble and thinks he can fly like a bird, but you need not worry about your father. On the contrary it is your father who worries about his children."

Seth and Mary, two servants, followed closely behind as they stopped outside a chamber door. "You can rest here, Father, where you can bathe and change clothes," she said. "There is fresh fruit and nuts next to the bath. Seth and Mary will assist you with anything you may need." Zia nodded to the servants, who politely bowed their heads at Bubba. "I am glad that you are alive, Father.

Rest now and we will call you when dinner is ready."

Zia and Dante continued down the corridor. Seth opened the chamber door. Bubba entered, followed by the two servants. Bubba stopped just inside the door and turned toward the male servant. He gently put his staff on the servant's chest, turning him around and marching him back outside with the staff on the center of the servant's back. The other servant followed.

"Thank you," he told the servants and closed the door.

Outside the main chamber of the room was a large marble pool full of swirling water filtering down overhead from the indoor spring like a waterfall. Next to the pool was a fresh change of clothes and new sandals.

After bathing, Bubba put on fresh clothes but elected to wear his old sandals. When he finished dressing, Bubba walked into an adjoining chamber that had been prepared in anticipation of his return. Over a large feathered bed, adorned with white linen and giant pillows, hung a huge oil painting of Lucy. Bubba moved close to the painting and stood motionless, his eyes fixed on the painting. Lucy was standing in a garden, holding a basket full of vegetables. Her eyes seemed to be reaching out, alive, talking, but still on canvas.

"Do you like it?" asked," Zia, standing at the door.

"Yes," Bubba said without taking his eyes off the painting. "I like it very much, especially her eyes. They are the color of the sea, and capture the very essence of her soul. Who could have painted such a picture?"

"Your daughter, Makia," said Zia. "She painted it. Who else could have done such work but someone who knew and loved her? The oil is still wet. She just finished it and put it in this chamber for you tonight. We plan to hang it in the main room. But we all agreed not to talk about Mother tonight. I am full of anger. My heart is sick from her loss and I often cry when I am alone. The king sits alone in his castle with no visitors from his family. I have forbidden the grandchildren to visit him. We will curse him until the day he dies and spit upon his grave."

"You must forgive him," said Bubba.

"How could you ever forgive such an evil act?" snapped Zia. "You loved mother more than us."

"Your hatred for the king will only destroy you. Only through forgiveness will your wounds be healed. I am sure, as we speak, the king suffers in his own right. Only God can avenge. Let my family, my children hold no anger against the king. Anger only destroys the soul, diminishes the mind and the heart, and separates one from God. Both your mother and your sister, Anna, now abide in the house of the living God."

Zia was taken back by the words of her father. She took her father's hand. "You, Father," she said with a slight childish giggle, "the one who thinks he has wings, often surprises me by such wisdom. Come now, dinner is ready. Everyone is waiting."

Outside the night air was cool. A fall wind stirred just enough to drift into the windows of the palace and flicker the candles on the dining table. A gentle rain was falling and a hint of thunder echoed in the distance.

The grand dining room was huge with two large fireplaces and stone pillars supporting the ceilings. A long marble table seated twenty guests. The heavy high-back chairs were made of solid mahogany and cushioned with soft leather, each having the Canite symbol embroidered on the back. The oak walls, reaching a good twenty feet from floor to ceiling, held many of Makia's art works.

A solo harpist played while the cooks prepared

roasted lamb, clams, and an array of fresh bread and vegetables. Zia did not want the evening spoiled. She had cautioned everyone to refrain from discussing their mother's death or to mention the king. There were still issues and resentments about Lucy's death the children had not resolved among the family members.

The evening was very amiable with small talk and pleasant conversation until Makia showed her paintings to her father. Some of the more abstract work made no sense to Bubba, but he and the others at the table listened with interest as Makia explained her concept of art.

One painting in particular stood out to Bubba. It was a painting of Kismira. Bubba was impressed by the details in the painting, right down to the trim on the watchtower where the family stood and watched the Canites arrive well over two decades ago. In the foreground was a small girl with blond hair standing alone by the seashore.

"Why is Anna standing alone?" asked Bubba.

"She is the not subject of focus," replied Makia.

"The shadows across the landscape reflect a sunset. Anna holds a single sand dollar in her hand. That is the way you remember Anna, the very last time you saw her alive. Yet, you left Tonka out of the painting. He was on the beach that day."

"Tonka was further down the beach with me," Makia explained with a quiver in her voice.

"Anna stands alone because you still see her alone like the day she was lost at sea. And on the contrary, she is the focus of the painting. You have erased the memory from your mind but you have failed to erase it from your heart. Everyone has forgiven you except you."

All eyes rested on Makia, waiting for an intellectual response. But now she tried to keep her composure as a tear ran out of the corner of her eye and down her cheek.

"It is time you forgave yourself."

Makia lowered her head and covered her mouth with a napkin.

"You have upset her, Father," replied Michael. The dinner table is hardly the place for such issues."

"I am sorry you think dinner is more important than your sister's welfare, but fine food and music will always be here while your sister may not."

Makia wiped her tears and looked at her father across the table. "My nightmares have stayed with me over the years and I often smile when I am not happy. And still the voice in the sea, my sister's cry, comes back to haunt me. I have often thought about spilling my own blood to rid me of the memory."

Zia and Celeste looked across the table at one another, surprised she had made such a statement when they thought there were no secrets between them.

Bubba held an outstretched hand to Makia. "Please, Makia, come to your father who now needs you as much as you need him."

Makia stood and walked to Bubba, taking his hand.

"Yes, Father," she said, kneeling down beside him. "Only you seem to know how much I have suffered."

The servants stood close by with food ready to serve, but Dante held up his hand in a gesture for the servants to wait while everyone at the table looked upon Bubba and Makia.

Bubba gently placed his hand on the side of his daughter's face.

"By the power given to me, you shall suffer no more, but only because my power comes from the one and only living God who relieves your suffering and forgives you as you now forgive yourself."

Makia raised her eyes at her father. Her lips trembled, and her eyes became alive and sparkled. She slumped, almost falling backwards but held onto her father's hand.

"You are being cleansed by the spirit," replied Bubba.

In a few moments she raised her eyes at her father and said, "I love you." Makia struggled to her feet and looked around the table. "What are you all looking at?" she asked.

No one could find the words to reply. They sat dumfounded and watched as Makia walked around the table, almost bouncing as she walked, while all eyes followed her. She flopped down in her chair like a child would do, turned and smiled at Dante and said, "Let's eat."

"Are you well?" asked Zia.

"I am very well, and why shouldn't I be?" replied Makia.

Dante motioned for the servants to bring the food.

Her sisters breathed a sigh of relief the ordeal was over. Zia shrugged her shoulders at Celeste. Celeste gave Zia a perplexed look.

Zi proposed a toast to his father just to break the silence and to put everyone back at ease. After they had toasted, dinner was served.

Fabia turned her lips to Zi's ear and whispered, "Your sister put on a good show, and so did your father. They were only looking for attention. That only makes me detest your family even more."

Zi acknowledged her comment by nodding only for argument's sake and looked at Zia.

Zia was watching Fabia when she whispered into Zi's ear. She guessed the whisper was a ridicule of Makia. Fabia confirmed Zia's suspicions by smirking at Zia and then at Makia.

Zia was relieved that the dinner quickly turned festive. The incident was quickly forgotten by everyone except Dante, who kept an eye on Makia the remainder of the evening.

Makia was normally reserved, an intellectual whose designing skills had helped Dante create the palace. Now she was acting like a child. She was talkative and laughing out loud for no apparent reason. Dante thought she was totally out of character and it puzzled him. He was a military man, astute to behavior patterns, methodical in his thinking and was always aware of things others didn't notice. He considered the option Bubba had cast some kind of hypnotic spell on Makia, but he did not dispel the notion Bubba might have actually healed her. Nevertheless, Dante engaged the dinner party, enjoying the evening, waiting for the right moment to question Bubba about his trip to Alabama that might shed some light on Makia's behavior.

Bubba eagerly listened to humorous stories about his grandchildren and now wished he had visited them more often. But he had always remained a recluse, a mystery to the Canites, who considered him an eccentric with more money than the king. By his arrival on foot in his tattered clothes, he had dispelled any notions about his wealth to the Canites.

Dante, Bubba learned over dinner, had taken over the affairs of the king, and now had an army that numbered more than ten thousand soldiers. The king had secluded himself in his chambers and seldom spoke to anyone.

Although the Canites had settled into a peaceful existence, Dante explained to Bubba there was friction between the Canites and the Egyptians over shipping tariffs, and trouble was on the horizon.

All his children held important positions within the Canites except for Celeste, whose business was having children. She and her husband Blithe, a merchant, now had six children, the youngest of whom was a girl only one year old.

Makia's husband, Saul, was a merchant marine and had done very well selling his goods to the Canites . . . of course with the help of Zia, the matriarch of the family who made sure all the family prospered.

Bubba had seldom talked with Blithe or Saul, and he was pleased to get the opportunity. It had taken Bubba well over a decade to be seated with all his family even if an unfortunate fate of circumstances had brought him there. Over dinner, his thoughts drifted to God, and he silently thanked God for reuniting him with his family and restoring his sanity.

After dinner, while an array of desserts made with honey, dates and yams were served, the question Zia feared would spoil the evening was raised by Dante.

"I have heard about your journey to Alabama," said Dante. "My surveyors cannot find this place anywhere on their maps. I have never heard of it."

"And you probably never will." said Bubba. "It is very far away and beyond the common imagination."

"What do people do there?" asked Fabia, with a smirk on her face and with a condescending tone.

Bubba rolled his eyes upward in a thoughtful gesture as though the question was difficult. After thinking for a moment, he turned his eyes at Fabia and said with a jest, "They play with coconuts."

The room burst into laughter. The harpist who had been playing and also listening, struck an off-chord.

Zia rolled her eyes and gave a deep sigh. "Oh,

Father," she said, "now everyone does think you are crazy!"

After the laughter subsided, Bubba looked around the table as though he was addressing everyone and all eyes came to rest on Bubba.

"My journey," said Bubba, "would be impossible to explain. But I will say this much. I have looked into the face of God and heard His voice. He is a God of love. He is a God of kindness, compassion, and forgiveness. Do not let fine silver, gold, or riches distort your values. We now eat good food, but I say to my children, it is better to share bread with friends if bread is all you have rather than eat fat oxen with enemies. And when you have only a slice of bread and are hungry, give it away and you will no longer be hungry. For tomorrow you will awake and find a wheat field on your doorsteps. The true blessings in life come from giving and not receiving. To know the true and only God transforms the person into a new creature, and everything that is old passes away. And from this transformation life on earth actually begins."

Most everyone at the table gave a respectful nod. Dante rubbed his chin and leaned back in his chair, contemplating the words Bubba had spoken.

Fabia broke the silence. "Did you learn this in Alabama, to give away everything and join the peasants and common people?"

Bubba answered, "There is nothing wrong with providing for the family, Fabia. It is the misuse of wealth that distorts true values. And my answer is yes. Give everything away to the poor, except for your basic needs. The true treasures in life are not found on earth but in Heaven."

"I will start with my dessert," she laughed, handing her dish to a servant.

"This God that you speak of," said Dante. "You call him the living God. You say you have spoken to Him, and He to you. I do not wish to argue but only want to be enlightened, but now my wife kicks me on the shin underneath the table to hush me."

The room once again burst into laughter.

"I did not want this to be a serious evening, Father," said Zia, cutting her doting eyes at Dante. "But Dante doesn't know when he has said too much, and often the wine does the speaking for him."

Dante spread his arms in a joking gesture. "Where did I find such a wife? She talks to me like the peasant one moment and the next moment she treats me like a king."

"You are not alone, Dante," replied Zi with a laugh. "I have always wanted many wives, and now with Fabia I have many. She has a dozen different personalities, one for each day. She is like having a dozen wives."

"You cannot make one wife happy," snapped Fabia, "much less many wives. Perhaps you need to learn to fly like your father. The two of you are very much alike."

"You dare to disrespect my father," Zia said very angrily. "I tolerate you only because you are married to my brother. You have been nothing but a problem to everyone since the day we met."

"You or your sisters have not one ounce of royal blood yet you expect to be worshiped like a god," retorted Fabia. "You have turned my brother into nothing but a sheep and made a mockery of my father."

"And you, Fabia," said Zia, "I would like to tear your heart apart to show everyone there is nothing inside but sour wine and bitter grapes."

Dante slammed his cup on the table, spilling his wine. He stood, pointing an angry finger at Fabia, raising his voice, and now directing his comments to everyone. "I am tired of the hatred and the resentments my family harbors between themselves. Tonight it shall be ended. I believe the man who sits before us has indeed seen the face of God and speaks the truth. I would like to hear more of what he has to say."

The room fell silent. Dante sat down, turning his eyes on Bubba. Zia could not believe the words came from her husband, Dante, who had never believed in anything other than himself. Fabia's stunned expression said that she was even more shocked by her brother, the decorated warrior, the arrogant man among men who seldom listened to anyone's opinion other than his own.

"I am sorry if I have disrespected you, Dante," said Zia. She looked around the table, addressing everyone and said, "We shall listen to my father."

Bubba paused for a moment, took a drink of water, and looked at Zia and then at Dante. "I did not come here tonight to lecture my children," said Bubba. "I am old but not yet feeble. I have heard the whispers behind my back. I have heard the jokes about myself being able to fly. I am not insulted. In fact, I find you all quite amusing. You bicker among yourselves over trivial matters, thinking it is I who is lost. My sandals are worn from walking many miles, but only I have walked in these sandals and expect no one else to understand why I choose to keep them when I was offered new ones. No one has the right to judge another because they have not walked in their sandals."

Fabia rolled her eyes at Dante, indicating she was bored listening to Bubba. Dante gave his sister an angry nod she had seen before, and she quickly looked the other way.

"For every rose that grows there is a thorn,"

continued Bubba, "and for every flower, there is a weed that grows beside. Where good exists, so does evil. And where there is hatred, love can also be found. Now is time to mend the soul and to heal the heart. Tonight the power of God's love shines down upon us so all may witness."

"Fabia is a beautiful person," continued Bubba. "I see the sunlight in her eyes and the sunset on her heart."

Fabia turned her eyes on Bubba, surprised she was the subject of his talk. She now listened to what he had to say.

"Fabia meant no harm toward me," he continued. "Her remarks come obviously from an unhappy marriage and loss of any authority she might have had before Zia became princess. In order to love Fabia you must first understand her. And to understand her is to love her. She has never had a father who truly loved her. And in turn she finds it difficult to express her love. But now I say to everyone seated here tonight, I love Fabia like my own children because she is a child of God."

Fabia's eyes filled with tears.

Bubba turned his eyes to Fabia and held an outstretched hand. Fabia hesitated for a few moments, then rose from her seat. She walked to Bubba while all eyes followed her in disbelief. She knelt beside Bubba and raised her eyes to his.

"How do you know so much about me?" asked Fabia. "We have never talked. Yet you say that you love me. No one has ever loved me."

"I say now to you, Fabia, for all to witness, I would lay down my life for you if the time should ever come. Within you dwells the spirit of God and an inner beauty waiting to manifest itself."

Fabia burst into tears and laid her head in Bubba's lap. "How can you love me when I did nothing but disrespect you?"

Bubba put his hand on Fabia. "You are very easy to love because I understand your suffering."

Zia and her sisters could not believe what they were witnessing. Zia thought Fabia was putting on an act to equal Makia's to make a fool of her father. Everyone at the table remained in a state of shock that Fabia would bow to anyone — much less their father — but now they began to reconsider their previous notions about her.

Michael, who had never believed his father's stories about the dark forest and the great sea, watched in awe as Fabia cried on his lap and now considered the notion that perhaps his father could actually sprout wings and indeed fly.

Both Dante and Zi looked at one another across the table. Zi raised a curious eyebrow at Dante. Dante wore a blank expression and quickly diverted his eyes back to Bubba and Fabia.

No one had ever seen Fabia bow to anyone, much less cry in public or show her emotions openly.

Dante looked at Bubba. "My sister never bows to anyone. Now two have knelt beside you and been transformed. You have the power of the Gods."

"I have no power unless it has been given unto me by God," said Bubba. "I certainly have no claim to Fabia's conversion but can only say that love is the only power in the universe that can heal a wounded heart. With Makia, a glorious act of God passed before your eyes without anyone taking serious notice. And even Makia is not fully aware she was healed tonight. Everyone thinks she is giddy from wine, but she is drunk from the spirit that renders the body, mind, and spirit into His submission. I wear the sandals I wore when I spoke with God, and the power of his supreme light still rest within."

Bubba tilted Fabia's face upward and looked into her eyes. He placed his other hand gently on her head and stroked her hair. "Fabia has now been reborn into the spirit of God, and only by the grace of God do her tears flow freely. My words were from the heart. I truly do love her and by love she now kneels beside me like a child and weeps. Tonight, Fabia has become a new person only by the power of love."

Everyone at the table remained speechless. Not another word was spoken until everyone had left and Bubba retired to bed.

Later that night Dante paced the floor of his bedroom. He had been awake most of the night, contemplating the power of the words he had heard. He walked to the window of his bedroom and looked out over the city of Canna. The sun was just climbing over the hills of the city and the rain now slowed to a slight drizzle.

Zia moved to Dante, putting her arm around his waist as he stared in the early morning sky.

"What did the sisters talk about in private after dinner?" asked Dante?

"You would find it hard to believe, my dear husband."

"I would believe anything after tonight."

"Let's just say my sister, Makia, is no longer the person she was. She has drastically changed. It was like all the burdens of the world have been taken off her heart."

"And my sister's eyes shone like the rising sun. Her face was aglow like a candle. Never have I seen her make such a transformation. Upon leaving, she said that she loved me. She has never said that before."

"And what did you say to her, my beloved husband?"

"I told my sister I loved her also, something I have never said to her."

"Perhaps there is such a thing called the power of love my father spoke of," replied Zia.

"Last night I was a witness to two miracles. Now I find myself witness to another."

"And what miracle is that, my dear husband?

"My own transformation," replied Dante. "No longer will the Canites worship many gods, Zia, but only the one your father spoke of. I have no doubt the wings of the angels took him to Alabama."

When Zia heard her husband speak with such conviction, tears swelled into her eyes. "Your words now transform me. Perhaps we can discover the same God together, just like my parents did."

"Yes, I would like that very much, my beautiful wife," he said, turning from the window and putting her arms around Zia. "Today is the beginning of a new life together."

The following morning, Bubba waited for his grandchildren on the cliff where he and Lucy had spent most of their precious moments together, praying and worshiping God. Fabia agreed to gather all his grandchildren and bring them to him, and he patiently waited. He sat upon his favorite rock with the autumn sun in his face while a gentle breeze from the ocean below stirred the many memories within him. He looked out upon the clear blue of the Mediterranean Sea and the great winding river, Euphrates, that had left the sea, cutting its path through the countryside in search of its own home. He and Lucy had named it Euphrates, meaning the river of life. At night they often listened to the river as the wind and seas seemed to give the river a life and soul of its own that echoed its own voice across the hills and valleys. Across the river he could see the busy city of Canna, which represented to him both life and death . . . a civilization with hope and life but misguided by sad misconceptions of sin and weighed down by the denial of the true and living God. He hoped and prayed Dante and Zia would lead their people in the ways of God, and his words would one day help them find truth within their hearts. Below him lay the ashes of his home, a reminder nothing on earth is permanent, the ashes but a consequence of his own misjudgment and wrong-doing. Above was a clear, beautiful sky with a warm yellow sun covering a bounty of endless pristine beaches and unspoiled countryside.

Bubba reached up and broke a leaf from a tree and twisted it in his fingers, examining it. In a simple leaf he saw the face of God because God had created it, and the leaf was just a small reminder of the great and marvelous world God had created.

He had come a long way since the dark forest, and now he wondered why, when God had so many from which to choose, that he — a common man, uneducated and with many physical defects — had been chosen to fulfill a divine destiny. He would soon answer his own question when Fabia arrived with the grandchildren, but now he opened his arms to Heaven and gave thanks unto God. When he had finished, the Heavens opened up and he was embraced by the great and wonderful light of God. He struggled off the rock, onto his knees, and lifted his eyes toward the light, listening to the voice within.

"With you, Bubba, I am very well pleased again," said God. "A few simple words from you have already changed the hearts of a few and one day many souls will be changed as a result. Sometimes it only takes a single holy thought embraced by only one heart to change an entire civilization."

"I did not expect this visit," uttered Bubba, "but I am overjoyed you now speak to me."

"I am always full of surprises," said God. "When I hear sincere prayer and devotion it is hard for me to resist the temptation of a visit. Although you are old in years, you come to me as a child, as I wish all my mortal children would do. But now listen to my message."

Bubba nodded his head. "Yes, Father, I am here to listen and abide in your presence."

"Fabia is eager to learn," continued God. "Speak first of the things you have learned to her. She will one day continue your work on earth and while you abide in my kingdom. There will be more that Fabia will teach that will lay the foundation and make ready for my beloved Son, Jesus, when He will one day carry the cross that will bear the sins of the world. Mortal man is easily lost in a world that seems unjust and suffers the consequences of the forefathers. But man will not suffer once he understands I am a Father of love, compassion, and forgiveness, and further learns to communicate with me through sincere prayer and devotion as you have done. Go forth now with Fabia and teach her all you have learned, and one day we will meet in my house where I have a lot of surprises for those who enter. Now peace be with you until we talk again."

The great light of God disappeared. As before, the light of God contained so much spiritual energy Bubba felt it pass through every square inch of his body. It was mesmerizing, rejuvenating, almost electric . . . but tranquil and peaceful, rendering him almost paralyzed for a few moments.

There were many questions Bubba wanted to ask God but knew life was in itself a discovery process and all of his questions would be answered in time. He was overjoyed by the fact God had briefly spoken to him. When his eyes adjusted to the natural light, he saw Fabia and his grandchildren standing before him. Fabia had the children take seats in the soft, comfortable grass surrounding the rock and then hurried to Bubba, kneeling down beside him.

"Are you well?" she asked. "Your eyes are like fire and aglow. Your face radiates like the sun."

Bubba reached out and took Fabia's hand, holding it tight. Fabia almost became faint by the transfer of spiritual energy from his hand to hers.

"Do not try to speak," said Bubba, "but only listen to the voice of God within your soul."

Fabia could only look into Bubba's eyes that were filled with the spirit of God, shining like a beacon into her own. In a few moments she regained her composure and uttered, "I feel as though I am drunk with wine."

"It is the spirit of God flowing freely within," said Bubba. "From this day on, you will drink only from the water of life and continue His message for all to hear."

"I am not well liked by anyone," Fabia struggled to say. "Why would God choose me?"

Bubba replied, "I ask you, Fabia, why not?"

* * * * *

Bubba's grandchildren now numbered eighteen. He had grandchildren to whom he had seldom spoken, but he could call every one by name. When they were seated a young girl about five years of age stood and spoke.

"What is the bird's name, Grandfather?"

"His name is Gork," replied Bubba. "He is a most unusual bird. He has been with me most of my life."

"Can we play with the bird?" she asked.

"Yes," said Bubba. "Gork loves children. But first tell me your name."

"My name is Anna," she replied, "but, Granddaddy, you already know my name. I am the daughter of Makia."

Tears swelled in Bubba's eyes.

"What is wrong, Grandfather?" asked Anna.

Bubba gently took Gork from his shoulder and placed

him on Anna's hand. She looked at the bird and smiled at her grandfather.

"There is nothing wrong," said Bubba, stroking Anna's face with his hand. "You just remind me of someone I once knew and loved."

Anna took Gork to the younger children and they played with Gork while listening to their grandfather. Bubba asked each child to stand and give their name and say who their parents were.

One stood and said, "Grandfather, I am Lolita, daughter of the great Princess Zia. You know my name so why do you ask who I am?"

Bubba replied, "I know who you are, Lolita, but I like to hear it from your own lips, as the Father in Heaven knows my name, but likes to hear me say it."

When they had finished repeating their names, Bubba spoke. "I shall say first there is only one God, the living God, and this God is your Father and he loves you. There are many things your parents forbid you asking, but with your grandfather you are free to ask what your heart desires.

Jeremy, the son of Celeste stood with a challenging voice and asked, "We have heard that you have spoken to God and He has spoken to you. What does he look like?"

Jeremy then took a seat, looking at the other children with a smirk and as though he had asked a question that could not be answered.

Bubba replied, "He looks just like you, Jeremy."

"Come now, Grandfather. How could he look like me?"

"He also looks like me," said Bubba. "He looks like Anna. He looks like all my grandchildren, and everyone in the world. All of us were created in His image. Each one of us is like a raindrop, and together we all make up a sea and within the sea is the face of God, because his spirit prevails within everyone of us."

When Jeremy heard this he lowered his head, realizing his grandfather was wiser than he realized.

Zelda, a girl of five stood and spoke. "We heard that you were real loony. Are you really crazy as many say?

Bubba chuckled. The children giggled.

"Zelda," Bubba said, "you are the youngest daughter of Celeste. You are very much like your mother. She also thought I was, like you say, loony."

All the children laughed again and became very comfortable with their grandfather, who said, "It is important you all laugh and have a good time. Humor and laughter are very good for the heart and the soul."

Another grandchild stood. His name was Gabriel, firstborn son of Zia and Dante. "I am very glad you have returned, Grandfather. You told us to be honest. I am very well to the point. I do not disrespect you, Grandfather, but even my mother says that you are not like the rest of us. Your feet are webbed and your fingers are funny. Some say you walk like a duck."

The children burst into laughter.

"Yes, Gabriel," Bubba said with a laugh, "I am glad you are like your mother, Zia. She is also outspoken and to the point."

Susannah, the nine-year-old daughter of Celeste, stood and asked, "Can we see your feet, Grandfather?"

"Yes," said Bubba. "I have walked many miles on my feet. More than you could ever imagine."

Bubba removed his sandals and showed the children his feet. While the children gathered around and studied his feet, Bubba explained, "My feet were a gift from God, and my fingers were the same. They have taught me some valuable lessons. But hear the words I speak to my beautiful grandchildren: Judge no person by your own standards, and never judge another by their outward appearance. True beauty lies within the heart. For within the heart is where the true treasures in life are found."

Gabriel heard these words and quietly sat down to listen more about what his grandfather had to say.

Bubba stood up and raised his arms as if he was gathering the children, who were now attentive to his every word.

"I have a great story to tell," said Bubba. "It's about a place I call the dark forest, and about a lion named Tonka, and the great sea where I was saved by God. And when I have finished, go tell the story to your parents. I shall begin my story in a place God sent me called Alabama."

Bubba was sitting on his stump, looking at the ashes of his burned home, when he saw Gork rise over the cliff and soar with lightning speed toward him. His eyes followed Gork until he was at Bubba's feet, flapping his wings and croaking. Bubba wondered why Gork was so excited. He watched Gork fly back to the cliff and circle. It was then Bubba saw the figure standing on the cliff and looking down on him. He stood and walked a few feet for a better look. The morning sun was bright and he squinted his eyes against the sun. When the shadowy figure came into view, Bubba's hands trembled. Tonka gave a loud roar and disappeared from view. Bubba was so overwhelmed his legs went limp and he sat down on the stump to wait on Tonka to work his way down the trail.

In a few moments he saw Tonka at the bottom of the cliff running toward him. Tonka dashed past Bubba without breaking his stride. Bubba laughed and turned his head toward the seashore and watched Tonka gallop at full speed along the beach. Tonka ran a short distance, turned and headed back toward Bubba. When he reached Bubba he came to an abrupt stop, roared and shook his mane. He was panting hard and wagging his tail.

Bubba stroked Tonka and lifted his eyes toward

heaven in a thankful gesture. In that moment he fully realized the power of God, and remembered what God had said: "Miracles happen to those who choose to do my will."

Bubba and Tonka spent the day walking along the seashore and sitting on the cliff. Bubba hoped the day would never end. His friend had come home, and he savored every moment. The day would always be a reminder that the only thing that endures in life is love; good thoughts and memories can never be lost.

The sunset that afternoon seemed unusually long to Bubba. The sun hung over the sea, lingering to fall beneath the earth, although the stars were out, and Gork was already perched in tree. A gentle breeze drifted across the seashore and the river and sea stood calm. Bubba sensed his time with Tonka was near the end. He hoped one day he would see him again. As the last rays of a golden sun were slowly being overcome by the dark, Bubba said goodbye to Tonka. Tonka galloped toward the parting sun, leaped, and disappeared into the heavens.

.

ABOUT THE AUTHOR

As a photo-journalist with the Stars and Stripes, Kenneth David Mobley's feature articles have appeared in more than 100 national and international newspapers and magazines.

In earlier years, he worked in commercials, television, stage, and film while living in Hollywood, California, and New York City, and has written comedy for such notables as John Candy, Mel Brooks, John Belushi, Bill Murray, and most of the members of the original *Saturday Night Live* cast.

On returning to Georgia, he and his sister, Sheila, opened Military Card and Gift, Inc, where his greeting cards were distributed to military bases worldwide. *Bubba Goes To Alabama* is his debut novel.

A native of Coastal Georgia., he enjoys playing piano, cooking, and pursing his lifelong study of theology and metaphysics.

The author can be reached via email at kennymobley79@yahoo.com or by snail mail at P.O. Box 2496, Brunswick, GA 31521.

ALSO FROM THOMASMAX PUBLISHING

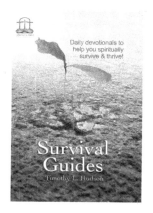

Survival Guides
By Timothy L. Hudson, $ 19.98

A verse from *The Bible* for each day of the year and a devotional reading to go with it from Timothy L. Hudson, founder of the University of Georgia Christian Campus Fellowship. Mr. Hudson has offered internet devotionals for many years, and this book collects 366 of his best. All author proceeds are donated to the UGA CCF. Unlike many devotional books that "preach to the choir," this book deals with real-life issues. Non-denominational. Makes a great gift, too!

IncrediBoy: Be Careful What You Wish
By Lee Clevenger, $ 12.95

To Christian Savage, 11, life is a cruel joke. He's the smallest kid in his class, unathletic, unpopular and a target for bullies. Worse, his brother is Mr. Perfect Boy, a star athlete and student. To escape life's cruelties, Christian resorts to daydreams, and in his favorite, he's a superhero he calls *IncrediBoy*. His life changes when he finds to rings lost by Yoqe, an evil man-eating alien, and he becomes ***IncrediBoy*** in real life. But Christian quickly learns that being a superhero isn't all it's cracked up to be. And though Christian doesn't know it, but Yoqe is on his way back to Earth to reclaim his rings. Can Christian's incredipowers defeat Yoqe? Or will Christian be the alien's next meal? Or could it be Christian has an un-incredible ace up his sleeve for his showdown with Yoqe? Ages 9 & up, includes "incrediglossary" to help young readers.

ThomasMax books are available almost everywhere books are sold and through internet sellers such as Amazon.com. If your favorite bookstore doesn't have the title you want, ask the store to order it for you. You may also order directly from the publisher at our website, thomasmax.com, using your credit card or PayPal account.

Printed in the USA
CPSIA information can be obtained
at www.ICGtesting.com
LVHW041540220923
758651LV00003B/53